Clocktower Books
San Diego

Have Blue

A historical novel
—Technothriller & Love Story—
Based on the true history of how
the F117A Stealth Aircraft
Was Invented and Saved the World

by

John Argo

Have Blue

By John Argo

Print edition available for order at your local bookstore. Also check for e-book editions designed for reading on all major digital platforms.

Clocktower Books
P. O. Box 600973
Grantville Station
San Diego, California 92160-0973
editor@clocktowerbooks.com
www.clocktowerbooks.com

HAVE BLUE

by John Argo

A Romantic Techno-Thriller based on true history

Dedication

This novel is dedicated to the staff at the Skunk Works who made the Stealth technology possible, especially the lateBen Rich. The real hero of the actual, historical story is the young Denys Overholser, who however declined to be interviewed for this book. The imaginary Paul Owens, and his intriguing fictional lady love, Marsha Kassner, therefore had to fill in—and did so quite well, I think.

This is a work of historical fiction, based on remarkable true history tale that deserves to be known by every American. Using the resources available to me, under time constraints, I chose to tell it as a fictionalized technothriller and a love story, with an entirely imaginary cast of characters. However, the true story of this history-changing aircraft's development will shine through. For the in-depth, true story, the reader's attention is directed to the nonfiction book <u>Skunk Works: A Personal Memoir of My Years at Lockheed</u> by Ben R. Rich with Leo Janos (Little Brown and Co., 1996). That work is an excellent source of informative reading on the real story of how this technology came to be.

Preface

This book is fiction, based on astonishing fact. The love story is an invention, as are the main characters and the Burbank suburb of Madeira. The background is real history—about how an obscure mathematician changed history and probably saved the world.

The most secret military project in U.S. history, after the Manhattan Project, was one called *Have Blue*.

As a result of the October 1973 Yom Kippur War, American strategic planners were horrified to realize that the world had nudged several steps closer to total annihilation.

On October 6, 1973, Egypt and Syria launched a sudden and massive attack from the north and the south, designed to destroy the Jewish state. The Arabs were supplied and trained by the Soviet Union, while the Israelis were being supported by the United States and several European powers. The Yom Kippur War represented a test of the superpowers' relative strengths and weaknesses.

Israel managed to halt the onslaught and turn the tables on the field of battle, routing her attackers. However, the Israeli Air Force lost 109 aircraft in 18 days of fighting. It seemed the Soviet Union had supplied their allies with invincible radar systems. American strategists analyzing these data came to the sobering conclusion that, if World War III were to begin, the United States Air Force would be shot out of the skies within as few as 17 days by radar-based defenses of the Soviet Union.

Was radar invincible?

If so, the next conclusion would be truly horrifying.

The United States was locked in a deadly embrace with the Soviet Union called MAD—Mutually Assured Destruction. Together, the two powers possessed about 50,000 nuclear warheads—enough to destroy much of life on earth. If either side launched first, the other side would retaliate in kind.

The safety of the world—the survival of mankind—depended on

the standoff between the two superpowers, in which both sides remained frozen and unable to act. The Yom Kippur War punched a hole in this concept big enough to drive a world war through.

The United States rested its strategic plan on a three legged stool: long-range bombers, nuclear subs armed with missiles, and Intercontinental Ballistic Missiles (ICBMs). Of these three, only the bombers had the flexibility to carry either conventional or nuclear bombs.

If our bombers could no longer penetrate Soviet radars, then the first and oldest leg of our strategic plan was gone, and the stool must surely fall. The only two options left would be nuclear ones, in the form of our subs and ICBMs—the so-called nuclear "Doomsday Card."

An urgent call—and an extremely secret one—went out to the major aerospace firms. At the President's request, an all-out effort must be made to develop some kind of weapon—a coating perhaps?—that would make our bombers invisible to radar. So far, no effective deterrent existed. The major contractors submitted their bids and the deadline passed.

At the last moment, the project director at one of our most secret research and development facilities realized they'd been overlooked— because they were so secret that the top people in defense didn't even know about them. This was Lockheed's Skunk Works, which over the years has produced some of our most esoteric—and secret—aircraft, like the U-2 spy plane, the D-21 drone to overfly Red China, and the SR-71 Nighthawk that could cross the U.S. in less than an hour.

But the Skunk Works hadn't built an Air Force plane since the Korean War. The Skunk Works' biggest customer was the CIA—which, in a surprising turn of strategy, let Lockheed tell the top Air Force brass about the Skunk Works.

At that moment in history, a young mathematician, outdoorsman, and jet nose cone expert at the Skunk Works stumbled upon an arcane Soviet paper that contained the key to beating radar.

It's called Stealth, and the F-117A Stealth fighter (really a small bomber capable of dropping two "smart" bombs) made its debut in the Gulf War in 1991. The Stealth plane flew only two percent of the air missions but knocked out about 40% of the total targets during the war. The Stealth fighters did almost all the bombing raids in and around Baghdad, precisely placing their bombs—including the one that went right down the air shaft of the Iraqi Air Force ministry and knocked the Iraqi Air Force out of the sky within the first few minutes of the war.

The F117-A Stealth fighter is one of history's great success stories.

This novel is a fiction based on the wondrous discovery made by a young man engaged in highly secret research. In this story, which is a story, the fictional hero based on that true-life mathematician discovers something else—the beautiful widow next door, and her young son who loves model airplanes.

Have Blue

by

John Argo

Chapter 1.

Absorption. That was the key word, the pot of gold, the holy grail, the buzz of the industry. Something was up, something big.

As Paul Owens drove home from work at the Lockheed Skunk Works in Burbank, California on a November day, a youthful looking man of twenty-nine in a red Mustang convertible, the wind over the Southern California desert was cool as it ruffled his thick, dark-brown hair, which hung down to his shoulders.

He was anxious to get home because... because... what?

Absorption. No, not that. Something else. The other thing.

Paul was an expert in the obscure science of radomes—jet nose cones made of non-interfering composites that were transparent to radar; and inside the radomes was the jet's radar tracking system. Paul was the best there was at this arcane specialty.

The air was silent except for the droning of small aircraft taking off and landing at Burbank's airport. Paul listened to rock music until the news came on—more disaster 9,000 miles away—and then flicked the radio off.

He did nose cones.

He did radar.

The Government and Lockheed denied that the place where he worked even existed, and he had a clearance as high as almost any general's; though his need to know was narrowed down to the mathematics and physics of the field that was his passion.

From a distance, there was little to reflect the ugliness of the Vietnam War, which was beginning to wind down, or the growing boldness of the Soviet Union in challenging the U.S. and her allies everywhere around the world.

Burbank, home of Universal Studios and several other cinematic giants, might not exactly be Heartland, U.S.A., but there was a peacefulness in the air, an Americanness, a safeness from war and chaos. Slightly inland, irrigation machines turned slowly in desert oases where vegetables lushly bloomed. There was a plantation slowness about the valley as laborers moved slowly about the fields, picking lettuce or spinach or fat round red tomatoes by hand.

A sense of urgency propelled him along this evening, but he'd put the cause of that urgency someplace where he could retrieve it. His head was full of mathematical formulations as he drove slowly to the Burbank subsection of Madeira, population 4,500, a bucolic swath of country living amid the suburbs. Paul was one of the world's experts on airplane nose cone radars. It was his passion, and he worked on it 24 hours a day, 7 days a week. The subject was always in his mind, whether he was home or at the Skunk Works. Lately it was absorption. The Government was desperate to make nose cones and fuselages that would suck up radar signals, refusing to allow them to return to whoever had sent them, and thereby rendering an airplane invisible. Would a metal do it? A paint? A material? Though Paul worked on other things as well, this was lately his pet project. It was a problem worthy of him, though he did not think of it that way.

He nosed in to a parking spot in the Madeira strip mall on the main route.

He picked up a BLT with extra mayo at King's Deli. His stomach was rumbling, and he realized he'd forgotten that he was hungry. Packing the brown bag absently under one arm, he jogged lightly several doors down to the small post office. He entered its gloomy interior—the fluorescents were already on, and the counter was shuttered behind steel slats. Eagerly, he bent down and peered into the tiny glass window of Box 4509.

"Yes!" He dropped his bag on the floor and fumbled with the key.

"Oh no!" It was a yellow notice, saying that he had a registered flat—what did that mean?—a package or something to pick up, but the post office was closed, and he'd have to come back in the morning. Damn!

The ZIP Code of origin... He rushed to the table by the wall, flipped open the book there, thrashed his way through the pages, and traced down the blinding rows of tiny numbers...MIT! Yes! His precious translation of the Russian mathematical paper was there on the other side of this damn wall, and he touched the wall with both hands as if he could somehow make it go away. But reality intervened. He'd be back when this place opened in the morning. He could wait one more night! He'd take it to work and work on it there! Unless his boss, Steve Rossi, who reported to Ben Rich, told him otherwise. Which was unlikely, since Paul usually worked many hours of overtime each week.

Minutes later, he pulled into his driveway, glad to be home while it was still daylight for a change. As he got out, the stillness and the smell of river reeds made him smile to himself. He walked through his old ramshackle house, picked up a can of cola on his way, and parked himself at the table on the back porch. As he devoured his sandwich, nearly groaning with the pleasure of not being in pain with hunger, he stared about his domain. He was paid well for what he did, and he'd chosen this quarter acre of delight because it reminded him of his farm origins in Ohio. His home was one of a string of quarter acre lots along Madeira Road. The neighbors were well separated, with huge old willow and pepper trees for added privacy. Running along the backs of the properties was a wide, shallow stream bed that was usually almost dry except for a trickle. Having that touch of wilderness added to the isolation and privacy he liked.

Much of Paul's backyard was waist deep in wild grass and oats. One day, he supposed, he'd have to get someone over to trim it. But what was the use, he thought, it would all grow back again. He thought again about his package. From the preliminary abstracts he'd read, he had a feeling that paper—by a Soviet professor, no less—might contain a clue in this maddening puzzle. Jeez, even the Nazis had toyed with the idea of radar-absorbent coatings during the last desperate days of World War II. They had designed and tested a remarkable V-shaped flying wing coated with materials that deadened the radar signal. Had the war continued a few more years, they might have found the complete answer, and then he, Paul Owens, would be chewing on some other problem today! He laughed to himself. Belching, he wandered over to the weather-beaten cupboard at the end of the porch, undid the padlock, and spread open the doors. There was his entire model airplane kit— enough to open a model airplane shop if he had time for such stuff. No, this was serious business. He'd loved these things since childhood— even had some engines dating back to his dad's fascination with the same hobby—but lately he'd been using his hobbies to help in his work.

The cupboard was full of tools, wings, fuselages, repair patches, dopes and paints and glues, oil, screws, model railroad parts (his other hobby)—and two working, radio-controlled planes.

Idly, he picked up one of his airplanes. He opened the tiny engine screw, poked an oil can nozzle inside, and squeezed the little can until the see-through indicator on the engine showed full. The engine took about as much oil as a fountain pen held ink. He closed the screw and wiped the engine with a red mechanic's rag. Adjusting the choke, he gave the propeller a good flick. The engine gave a healthy *sput!*—good compression.

He picked up the control, pulled the antenna fully out, and checked the battery. The juice was fully recharged.

Moments later, he stood just away from his back porch, controls in hand, watching his two-foot wingspan Condor buzzing over the high grass like a strange white dragonfly with black lettering.

It took him a minute or two to become aware of a child's voice speaking excitedly nearby.

Chapter 2.

Marsha Kassner, thirty, heard her son Peter, 9, yelling excitedly, and she heard a faint buzzing sound. They had moved in only a week ago, and she was still leery of who her neighbors might be. Wiping a glass with her dishcloth, she stepped onto the back porch. These houses were very old, and unlike most Southern California houses, they had front and back porches from the days when people were more sociable.

What an odd sight, she thought. There was Mr. Owens, the man next door, standing in his back yard with a hand control. He had a model airplane flying in circles over those horrid weeds of his. The real estate man had told her Owens was an okay guy—just really weird but harmless in the final analysis. The fact that he appeared to live alone and have no family or children did not quite sit well with Marsha, and she eyed the scene warily.

Peter, a solid little boy with straight dark-blond hair cut like a chestnut half on his sturdy head ran to her, pointing backwards. "Mom, look what that man's got. Can I go see?" He ran by her in a semicircle as if expecting to get her okay and continue in an unbroken path toward the mysterious Mr. Owens.

"Peter, you stop right there!"

"Aw Mom."

"We haven't met Mr. Owens yet. We don't want to annoy him." Inwardly, she thought—we don't trust him. We want to check him out and avoid that as long as possible. The real estate man said Owens worked at the big Lockheed plant, but that he never dressed up for work, and it wasn't clear what exactly he did. Wasn't an ordinary assembly line worker, far as he knew; made pretty solid money, from what he'd heard. Of course, real estate people would say anything to close a deal, she thought. Why did everything have to be so hard in life, she wondered.

Peter jumped up and down and hoarsely cried: "Mo-o-om!"

She understood his hunger; it scared her. Was it more for the magic of a motorized airplane, or the company of a man who might in some pale fashion imitate the wonder of the dad he'd lost? "Okay, honey," she said, setting the rag and glass down. She held out her hand and he took it eagerly. "Come on, let's go introduce ourselves."

She felt butterflies as she approached the end of her neatly clipped property. She halted at the rickety wooden picket fence—fresh white paint on her side, flaking ancient gray surface on his (she'd noticed the first day already, and it fit with the look of his house). "Hello!" she called.

Peter jumped up so his feet were on the 2-by-4 along the bottom of the fence. He leaned forward and hollered: "Hello, Mister!"

Chapter 3.

Paul shook his head lightly as he heard the voices coming toward him in a light wind. Seeing two figures out of the corner of his eye, he raised one finger to signal he'd be with them in a moment. Using both hands, he guided the plane in to a picture perfect landing near the fence, except that one wheel hopped into a gopher hole, and the plane tipped forward, its tail in the air.

Both persons by the fence clapped.

As he approached them, he saw that one was a little boy with excited eyes, and the other was a very attractive dark-haired woman who instantly made Paul feel awkward. "Thank you," he managed to stammer. He bowed slightly, as if he were in a ballet.

The woman and the boy laughed. She was tallish, with a nice figure. Her face attracted Paul the most—well proportioned, with a small gently ski-ramped nose, a lush sweet mouth still hinting of the day's red lipstick, dark eyes full of intelligence and mirth, and a high intelligent forehead. Her cheeks were wide and soft and rounded, her jaw line more squarish. Actually, he thought as he walked closer, she was knitting-magazine pretty.

They shook hands, and she had a dry, firm grip. Her fingers were soft, as if they were plump, which they weren't.

"I'm really sorry we're bothering you, Mr.—."

"Owens. Paul Owens. You're not bothering me at all."

"—My son—Peter—."

"—Call me Pete—."

"Okay, Pete."

"My son Peter loves things like airplanes and model trains and all. He just couldn't resist coming over. I'm sorry."

Paul lifted Pete over the fence. "No problem, Mrs.—."

"Kassner. I'm Marsha Kassner." She turned a little bit red. Her eyes followed her son in alarm as Paul set Pete down. The boy immediately ran over to the plane and started to pick it up. In the same moment, one of his fingers poked through the wing surface.

Marsha Kassner gasped.

Paul laughed quietly. "Easy, Pete."

The boy dropped the plane, hard, nose first, into the ground.

Marsha Kassner gasped again.

"It's okay," Paul said.

Pete sat by the plane, looking mortified. He looked at his mother for help, and at Paul to determine just how angry this new neighbor might be.

"I'll tell you what," Paul said. "For now, let me handle the plane. I'll teach you all about it as we go along, and pretty soon you'll be an expert. Okay?"

"I'll pay to get it fixed," Marsha Kassner said quickly. "Peter, you get over here right now!"

A tear dribbled down Pete's cheek as he hove himself upright.

"Easy does it," Paul said picking up the plane. "Tell you what. I have two of them. Mrs. Kassner, honest, it's nothing. I fix these things all the time. Let's get the other plane and I'll help you fly it for a few minutes." He took the wounded plane in both arms. "Wait here, okay?"

A few minutes later, Condor II circled in the air over the weeds.

Pete worked the controls, with Paul kneeling behind him, holding the box with the panel for him.

Marsha Kassner stood beside them, having stepped over the picket fence. She wore tight jeans, high tan suede boots, and a crisp cowboy shirt with pale, small blue checks. A nice looking lady, Paul thought; wow; ones like this were all taken; too bad.

"Easy," he told Pete. "We don't want to crash in that tall grass."

"Why?" Pete asked.

"Because that's full of radar nodes."

"What?" Pete asked, and his mom laughed.

"Seriously," Paul told her. "I'm a radar specialist. I know" (he laughed suddenly) "I should cut the grass, and I guess now I will have to. I bring my work home with me."

"What's a node?"

"I'll show you next time we see each other, maybe this weekend if I'm home and it's daylight."

"It's getting dark," Marsha Kassner said quickly, apparently taking it as a cue he wanted them to leave. Why did she keep doing that? He was enjoying himself. She smelled faintly of some citrusy perfume with violet and licorice in it or something.

"We'd better get home and let Mr. Owens put his plane away. I'm so sorry about the other one that he broke."

"No problem at all. I can dope that wing and have it fixed in no time."

Condor II came in to a smooth landing, guided by Paul. Marsha and her son clapped. She beamed. "That was magnificent."

He wanted to say something witty like "I'm generally thought of as magnificent" or maybe "that's as magnificent as I get, I'm afraid," but nothing came out.

He managed to stammer good-bye and shake Pete's hand as they left.

Thoughtfully, he rubbed his hand along the broken wing of Condor I. Funny how suddenly things happened. A stranger could come up and tear a hole in your wing or your heart and just not even realize what they'd done. For a few moments, he'd actually forgotten his Russian paper.

Chapter 4.

As Paul pulled out of his driveway, he spotted Marsha Kassner pulling out. Pete sat in the passenger seat, ready for school. They both waved, and Paul waved back. Marsha pulled away, and Paul sat for a moment enjoying the afterglow of the little smile she'd sent his way, the little flutter of fingers.

At 7:55 a.m., Paul stood outside the post office as Jane Hardiway, the postmistress, unlocked the doors. "Hello, Paul."

"Hello, Mrs. Hardiway." He waved the yellow slip. "You have a package for me."

The post mistress was an older lady, with gray hair and a round figure. She laughed. "Every time you get a package, you're here first thing in the morning like a schoolboy. You sure you're not getting some of those racy magazines?"

The several other persons present laughed.

He almost said: "No, I'd have that delivered to my house," but he realized then they'd laugh even more. Should he say "I don't read those magazines?"

She patted him on the shoulder. "You are as red as a tomato. I'm sorry. Come on, it's another one of those research thingies full of mathematical formulas. Might be alchemy, for all I know."

Too eager to drive to work immediately, Paul sat outside on the steps and tore open the wrapper. Out came his treasure—it still smelled of alcohol from the repro machine. He'd ordered this English translation from his old alma mater, knowing that if he ordered through Lockheed they'd hold it up for all sorts of security reasons, even though it was available in the narrow academic channels that understood this material.

There it was: "Method of Edge Waves in the Physical Theory of Diffraction."

Hmm, Paul thought, diffraction? Instead of absorption? Interesting.

"... by Pyotr Ufimtsev of Moscow." Translated by the U.S. Air Force Foreign Technology Division.

As he flipped through with trembling fingers, he quickly recognized familiar century old equations of Scottish physicist James Clerk Maxwell, which had then been worked on by German electromagnetics expert Arnold Johannes Sommerfeld. The body of these equations taken together would predict how the geometric configuration—the shape—of an object could affect—or deflect— electromagnetic radiation. Now Ufimtsev had taken these realizations a few steps further.

This wasn't what Paul had expected, but he was intrigued. Instead of absorption, diffraction? He frowned as he stared at the paper, beginning immediately to realize its implications. If you were trapped in a box, and the situation looked hopeless, perhaps you had to get out of the box completely and into another problem.

Diffraction, he thought as he drove to the Lockheed Advanced Development Projects division (the "Skunk Works").

Insistent squelches of a siren made Paul look into the rear view mirror. He saw the twirling red white and blue lights of a police car and frowned. He was doing 45 in a 50 mile and hour zone. What was going on?

As he pulled over, he wondered if this stop had anything to do with the emergency procedures worked out with key employees at the Skunk Works. Soviet spy satellites moved overhead daily, monitoring such details as the numbers of cars in the parking lots, and the identities of their owners. Soviet fishing trawlers in international waters monitored all radio and telephone traffic in Lockheed's sprawling facilities. There was little doubt that there might be land-based electronic spies around Burbank itself, perhaps working out of a trailer or from a hillside apartment—none had been caught, but Paul and the other employees had seen training films about it. Finally, Paul was one of about 100 top technical experts who had been through a seminar on emergency procedures, like what to do if you're kidnapped. Because of all this, Paul was less inclined to think he was being pulled over for traffic violations rather than some higher security issue.

The Sheriff's deputy who walked slowly toward Paul's car looked familiar—Toole something, Paul thought, waiting impatiently as he fretted about getting to work to review the new manual.

"Morning, Mr. Owens," said Deputy Jeff Toole, a big blond man of thirty who looked tough and competent. Toole put one hand on the Mustang's roof and leaned close. "Mr. Owens, no need to take out your license."

Paul relaxed a bit. "I wasn't speeding, was I?"

Toole shook his head. "Nope. How have you been, Mr. Owens?"

"Fine." What was this all about?

"Mr. Owens, I was speaking with Mrs. Burley, the town librarian, yesterday afternoon. I just happened to be getting some books to read to my two little kids. She was kinda kidding and kinda not kidding when she said she's about to send the law after you."

"Oh my God."

"Well, now, we're a small town here, and no need to panic."

"No, but I do have some books... Oh my God, it's been six months, hasn't it."

"That's what she says."

"I'll bring them to her tomorrow."

"Thanks, Mr. Owens. Sorry to bother you."

It was like a small town, Paul thought as he drove on. He'd checked out some special order UCLA texts on nose cone integrals some time ago.

He showed his ID to the guard at the Skunk Works, near the Burbank airport, and sprinted across the parking lot into Building 259. This was a long, narrow makeshift structure, almost like an oversized double-wide mobile home, with laboratories and offices on either side of a wide main corridor. This building connected to other buildings on the site via a warren of passageways. Paul's office was a small lab about 20 feet square with a fishbowl window overlooking the corridor and a tiny overhead window overlooking the parking lot.

He burst into the office, letting the door rock on its hinges as it quietly moved until it slammed loudly shut. He dropped the paper on his main design table and went to the fridge for a cold cola. Pulling up a bar stool, he resumed reading the Ufimtsev paper. Blindly, he groped for a pencil and a yellow notepad. Soon, he would stop every once in a while and pencil calculations on the pad.

Meanwhile, the office was steeped in silence except for the hum of the air-conditioning and the on and off sounds of the little refrigerator. The fluorescents buzzed faintly, and the three model airplanes hanging from the tiled ceiling swayed gently in a barely discernible breeze. Against one wall was a large wooden cabinet of pigeon holes, each of which contained as many rolled up blueprints as could be jammed in there. On a large central table, books and papers were piled, and through a maze of such mountains wound an H-O scale model railroad. Several large, ugly gray steel shelves held stacks of papers, a number of plastic model racing cars, and a paperweight from Aspen (Paul loved to ski, though he hadn't found time—or companionship—to go lately). The bulletin board, on another wall, was covered with a mix of work related notices and photo-duplicated jokes that everyone passed around the plant.

He would have to re-read this Ufimtsev paper several times, he realized, but he was already getting the general drift. The author turned from his general observations about the Maxwellian phenomena to the more specific proposal that one could use the surface structure of a flying object to optimize—or, rather, minimize—the object's radar return, its signature in the air. Paul frowned. This was a Soviet paper. Could there be trickery here? He painstakingly checked some of the simpler equations, and it sure looked as if the theory made sense. He threw his pencil down and looked at this notes. Damn, this would have to be tested. It sounded too good to pass up. He started to read again, underlining passages and equations that seemed central to the thread he was after.

The phone rang. On the other end was an engineer named Robert Latham, over in Production (on the main shop floor of the Skunk Works). "Hello, Paul? You've had the latest materials samples for three days now."

Paul slapped himself on the forehead. "Right! I'm sorry, Bob. I've been so busy I haven't had time to finish testing."

"Any luck so far?"

Paul glanced toward his model railroad. "Not really. If there's a change it's miniscule. I'll finish testing today and get the analysis back to you."

With a reluctant sigh, Paul put the tantalizing paper aside and flicked on some wall switches. The electric train made a snapping sound as juice flowed through the system. The long black steam locomotive was a beauty, with its matching coal tender. Paul had bought it at the same flea market in Madeira where he'd picked up the fridge. He couldn't resist also picking up a non-matching but intriguing string of four silvery streamlined AmTrak cars that belonged behind a diesel, not a coal-burner, but what the hey.

Paul flicked on a set of wall switches. Then he walked around the big table, to quickly check that the tracks were clear. Meanwhile the test equipment warmed up. Paul picked up the first of the postcard-sized rectangles that Bob had sent over, and installed it in a slot atop the locomotive. Checking to make sure that the test equipment was ready, Paul started the train around the table for a couple of test runs. The track was a large circle, with several sizable waves in it to make it interesting. The train ground through its paces at a slow speed. Paul made a few adjustments. The locomotive's head and rear lamps, and the passenger cars' windows, were brightly lit. A thin train of smoke poured from the loco's stack, and it uttered a few harmonious horn chords. Paul couldn't resist—he cranked it up to full speed. The train snapped through its turns like a snake on the way to its victim. Sometimes only the card, standing on edge atop the loco, was visible above the canyons of papers, books, and equipment.

Paul adjusted the radar screen on his right. It glowed green, an upright unit with its display at eye level, and the controls on a yellow steel piano board. Next, Paul checked the radar output, a second-hand CHP radar gun mounted in a wooden catapult frame. He calibrated the gun and aimed it at the middle of a square made of strips of red tape attached to the opposite wall 18 feet away. On every pass, the train moved through this rectangle. As it did so, it tripped a switch that sent a burst from the gun. So far, no matter what coatings Production sent over, the return was always above 85%—not a good showing, and Northrop was rumored to have far better materials. Rumor was they would get the biggest absorptive R&D and production award in history. There was little the Skunk Works could do at this point. Unless, Paul thought, there was something to that paper...?

One by one, Paul ran twelve cards through the process. His was only one of five different sections in which these cards were tested, and he was not tasked with really rigorous testing—just backup, in case he detected some anomalies. QA and RADAR Engineering were responsible for the detailed tests with higher power transmitters over longer distances, returning to more sensitive instruments.

Paul ran through his paces, wanting to get this behind him.

He realized he'd forgotten his cola, and it had grown a bit warm. He got two nice fat ice cubes from the fridge and dropped them in a glass, then slid the cola down the inner side to minimize fizz-loss. Then he cranked up some disco tunes, let the train whizz around smoking and whistling, and, using a regulation black U.S. Government issue ball-point pen, filled in the report papers on the dozen test cards.

"Paul!"

He looked up. There was his boss, Steve Rossi, who reported directly to Ben Rich. With Steve were three rather surprised men in suits. Two of the men were older, with very sour faces. One was younger, with an arrogant, supercilious face, and a perfect preppy look including a nearly shorn, grayish Marine Corps hair cut. Hair was a big thing these days, and Paul's tended to curl over his ears. It wasn't that he was a wannabe hippie so much that he didn't often find time to visit the barbershop. The three dour visitors were looking at his hair with visible revulsion, as if a leftist commie spy had invaded this inner sanctum.

Paul turned down the music. "Sorry. What's up, Steve?"

Steve pointed. "The train."

"Oh yes." Paul turned that off. "Well?"

Steve introduced the men. The young one with the attitude was Alex Fitch. "These gentlemen are Government auditors. Mr. Fitch is with the Air Force, and (he named them) are with the Defense Department."

One of the older men, who now shook out a cigarette and lit it with a click of his lighter, asked Steve pointedly: "Don't you people have a dress code in this place?" He pointed to the bulletin board. "Let me give you a friendly word of advice. Get rid of any personal pictures, jokes, or what have you. Making funny copies on Government equipment is a terminable offense."

The other older man now also lit up; same ceremony—shake out a long one, insert filter between yellowed teeth, and flick that Zippo. This man nodded to Steve. "You're going to be seeing more stringent inspections from now on. We're just here to give you fair warning. And make sure that young man gets a haircut. We don't need any damn long-hairs around here."

Alex Fitch walked around rolling his eyes and smirking. "Well. I think the airplanes are nice, Mr.—"

"Owens. Paul Owens." Paul waved his hand in front of his face as the smoke began to make him dizzy.

"Oh yes. I want to remember that name." He touched a plane with his index finger, and it rocked back and forth. "Nice. I think I did my last one when I was 14. When I discovered girls." Fitch walked around the table. "And the train, Mr. Owens? Do you have, like, children or something?"

Steve cleared his throat. "Mr. Fitch, Paul works up to 100 hours a week. He's a leading expert in his field. I think we can indulge him."

Fitch whirled. "Sure, I'm sorry. Hey, forgive the attitude. We're not here to be pals. We all have our jobs to do, and I want to make sure that we start out on the right footing." He looked at Paul. "Nobody is indispensable, Mr. Owens. Just remember that."

Paul was too stunned to laugh or retort. He now realized that Steve had looked pained to begin with, and he didn't want to add to his boss's discomfort.

"Let's move on to the next section," one of the sour faced auditors said. He turned back and said: "I better never hear that blasted hippie music again, pal. Take the radio home today. Do you read me?"

After they had left, with a chorus of thank yous and sour faces, letting the door slam shut, Paul sat on the stool with his heart beating rapidly. "Actually, it's disco, you stupid old buffalo," he said to the mute door. He rose in a John Travolta stance, one finger pointing up in front of him, the other down behind him, and keened: "Stayin' alive! Stayin' alive!"

He whirled and smacked the buttons on the test equipment to shut it down. "I can't believe this damn place! Where do they find these idiots?"

He repeated the question in Steve Rossi's office a half hour later.

Rossi, a snappy dresser in his mid-forties, with graying curly hair that had once been black, sat back. He wore a powder blue suit with wide lapels, a white shirt, and a kind of loud yellow tie with red circles in a mix of pop art and psychedelia. Small nuances of dress or tonsure could send enormous signals in these jumpy, crazy times with so much bitterness in the air about the war. Rossi wasn't one of "them," however.

Rossi, an ex-Marine Corps officer who'd quit after one tour in 'Nam to finish his Master's in Electrical Engineering, was a natural manager and he understood technical issues. Paul liked him a lot, and they got along.

"So where do they find these guys?" he asked Rossi.

"My friend," Rossi said genially, "you forget that we labor for the Government, which sometimes pays people to store their cheese in tunnels, or to not grow tobacco, or whatever, but at other times drops napalm on villages and water buffaloes. It is a crazy mistress we serve, and you have just seen her vent her wrath. It's their way of leaning on us, letting us know who's boss. Hell, they do inspections so strict they don't even do those in the military anymore these days." He grinned. "You apparently remind them of every college student they have ever hated. Congratulations on being young."

"That's my offense, huh? Do these guys know I have a high level security clearance? Do they know I don't smoke, drink, do drugs, or run red lights?"

"It's the hair. That's all they care about."

Paul sputtered: "Hippies! That's last decade! This is the Seventies! We're into disco now. Don't these cadavers know that?"

Rossi stood, pulled out his wallet, and dropped a ten on the desk. "Here. It's on me."

"What?"

"I'm ordering you to get a haircut. Today."

"But I've got work to do."

"I know how you feel, but this is work. Keeping these guys happy is part of our jobs."

"I'm not going to get my hair cut until I'm ready."

"We can't afford to lose you, Paul, but these jerks can pull the plug on you."

"Because of my hair?"

"This is the Age of Aquarius, pal. Hair is king. Hair gets you hired and fired. They don't care what's inside your head but on the outside of it."

"I'm not doing it." Paul added: "And guess what, Steve. I'm not working a minute more than eight hours today. I'm going home on time. Screw all the hours I put in."

"I love that morale," Rossi said sitting back and putting shiny black loafers on his desk. He lit a cigarette and blew smoke at the ceiling. "Take the rest of the afternoon off. Get a haircut. Go see a movie and forget all about it. Come in tomorrow and whistle while you work. We gotta build nose cones and save the world. Even with these dickheads sneaking around here. Believe me, it's only going to get worse."

At four p.m., Paul sat in a barber's chair in downtown Burbank. He'd had a grilled cheese sandwich and a strawberry milkshake and was about to buy tickets to see The French Connection. Still fuming, he'd decided to get his head shaved into a Marine Corps 'do. At the last moment, he remembered that he wanted to look good for Marsha Kassner; so he made it just a plain short haircut with no curling at the edges.

Chapter 5.

Paul walked down the street, math paper tucked under his arm, and enjoyed the sensation of wind blowing over his newly shorn scalp. The Southern California sunshine filled a cloudless blue sky and cast a restful air over what would otherwise be a horrible day for Paul. But Paul had confidence that Steve Rossi would work with Ben Rich to find a way to get these hard-asses off his back. Too early yet to panic.

Paul glanced at his watch. Ninety minutes until the movie began. He felt hungry.

On impulse, he walked into the nearest bar & grill, and ordered a steak. He sat on a corner bar stool, smelling the tantalizing aroma, and listening to the sizzle of the grill in an adjoining room of the shady establishment. Pulling out his pen, he propped the Ufimtsev paper before him and resumed his close reading. He pulled a pile of stacked napkins over—ignoring the bartender's raised eyebrows—and began working equations.

Yes, that had to be it—diffraction. Of course. Structural stealth had already made its way onto various planes—like the SR-71, whose long, sleek profile presented a very small front-end radar image—but this Ufimtsev paper pointed all the way.

The steak, fries, and salad came, and another crisp, cold beer. He munched absently, feeling his hunger lessen and go away. He belched absently as hands appeared out of nowhere and removed his plate. Another small 7-ounce beer appeared, and he sipped at that, feeling a buzz of deep comfort as he began sketching triangles on the napkins.

Suddenly he rose. "What do I owe you?"

The brawny black bartender eyed him suspiciously. "For the food or for the napkins?"

"Huh?" Paul stared at the pile of notes. "Oh. Sure, I'll pay for them."

"Just kidding. But next time." The bartender made lightheartedly threatening body language.

Paul paid and hurried out the door. The sunlight blinded him for a moment, and as he reached for his car keys, his hand encountered his movie ticket. He glanced at his watch. Damn it! Twenty minutes late. Never mind—he didn't have time to sell the ticket back either—that would have to wait for another day. He backed the car out from the curb-nose parking and headed home.

As he pulled into the driveway, he saw Marsha's car parked by her house.

Pete waved from the front porch, and Paul waved back.

Paul went inside his house and dialed the phone.

A woman's languid voice answered. "Yes?"

"Mrs. Garcia. Is Alberto home?"

"Yes, Mr. Owens. I'll get him for you."

A minute later, the young Guatemalan-American's voice came across. "Hello, Mr. P. How's it going?"

"Good, Alberto. I have a job for you if you feel like it."

"You got the money, I got the time."

"I want you to come by as soon as possible and mow my back yard."

"I'm on my way."

Paul took the Ufimtsev paper into the living room. The living room took up a good part of the west end of the small, two-bedroom ranch-style house, with windows on the west side overlooking Marsha's house, and openings—on the left, into the parlor and out the front door, on the right, into the kitchen/dining area and out the back door. The bedrooms and the master bath were on the east side of the house, on the other side of a structural wall that ran the length of the house. In the middle was also the hall that led out to the garage, which was stuffed to the rafters with Paul's bicycling, canoeing, skiing, and other sports apparatus, plus his hobby equipment. No car had seen the inside of that garage in years; but then this was Southern California, where people did not have basements or attics, and the garage served that purpose. The floors throughout the house were of bare wood. On a trip to Omni-Mart when he'd first moved in, Paul had picked up some knotted throw rugs in Santa Fe style soft pastels, and those were scattered here and there.

The interior of the house had a worn but cozy feel, and an atmosphere of dark, old wood. Paul felt comfortable with it, though he sometimes felt a little lonely, or bored, or something, and he wished he had time to buy more furniture so that the house wouldn't quite have that sole-occupant echoingness.

Quickly, Paul cleared the table of yesterday's dinner plate, plus stacked copies of non-classified professional magazines like *Nosecone Review*, *Aeronautics*, The Aero Engineer, and so on. He pulled out his newly acquired desktop calculator, a thing of beauty that did ten digits, ran sines, cosines, and tangents, Fourier Transforms, integrals and derivatives, and more—one of his prized possessions. One day far in the future, he thought, people would have small home computers much smaller than the huge mainframes that one had to build a building around. One of the reasons he spent such long hours at the plant was because of the computer access to the giant IBM OS 360 mainframe.

He began the tedious task—which the computer at work would do 100 times faster, if Rossi had let him stay at work today—of approximating the flight surfaces. He had an idea in mind of what this plane would look like, but he kept shaking his head with doubt. From the first sketches, this did not look like any plane he'd ever seen. It looked more like one of the fantastic flying machines in that new science fiction movie, *Star Wars*. It looked a bit ominous when viewed toward the front, like a preying mantis about to jump on the viewer and devour him. *But,* he thought, *cross one bridge at a time.*

He barely noticed the sudden burp of a lawnmower, the drifting aromas of blue smoke from a mix of oil and gasoline, and then the wet juicy hay smell of newly mown vegetation. The smell pleased him, distantly, because it was something from home that he associated with Spring and pleasure. But he kept right on working.

Sure, he thought, the right combination of structure and surface would multiply the diffraction effect many times over. It would remain for testing to determine just how significant. But it looked to him as if this configuration would do the trick. One day in the future, computers would be much more powerful, and he would design a plane that was all curves, with no flat surfaces to return a radar signal straight to its source. For now, with limited 1970s memory capacity, he'd have to settle for a configuration of triangular surfaces, all of them skewed at angles to each other to diffuse a radar signal.

The afternoon sun was getting wan, throwing long shadows, when there was a knock on the door. Paul got up to answer, feeling a crick in his back from hunching for hours.

The smiling young man's boisterousness was almost painful as it disrupted Paul's concentration. "Whassup, Mister P.?" Alberto grinned widely. He was a big kid of 18, wearing jeans stained green, and he swung a pair of ugly work gloves that looked soggy.

Paul gave him a check for twenty bucks and Alberto took off, waving gratefully.

Then another voice piped up. "Hey, Mr. Owens. What are you doing?"

Paul grinned. "Oh, hi, Pete. I'm doing my math homework. What are you doing?"

Pete tilted his head to the side and peered suspiciously from his side of the fence. "Adults don't have homework."

"Some do. Is yours done?"

"No. I'm stuck on long division."

"Want some help?"

Pete made a face. "Yeah, I guess. Hold on, I better check with Mom." He ran off in a whirl of legs.

Paul walked around the front yard, stretching.

Marsha appeared, smiling. "Hi." She looked uncertain. "Is Peter bothering you?"

"Not at all. I was going to help him with his arithmetic."

She warmed. "Oh, would you? That would be so nice."

"Send him over. We'll work in the living room. You can come over too, if you like."

He went into the house and tried as best as he could to tidy things up. Amazing, how one suddenly noticed the amount of disorder—like the ironing board that needed to be put away; and the basket of clothing that had now waited six weeks to be ironed...should have asked Mrs. Garcia if she'd been sick, because she normally came twice a month to clean and do laundry.

He spotted Marsha and Pete coming hand in hand. Yesss!

It wasn't that he was plotting to help Pete to see her, but he was glad she was coming over. She seemed everything a woman should be, he thought, and he couldn't figure out why that was. She was pretty, though not beautiful. She was warm, but not gushy or anything. She seemed a little distant, or darty like a jackrabbit, he thought, but maybe she was shy. Or, damn it, maybe there was a man in her life. Where was Pete's father? Who was Pete's father?

"Knock knock," she called.

"Screen door's open."

"What a nice house," she said sincerely.

Paul was embarrassed by the house's worn appearance. He wanted to say something like "aw, you're just supposed to say that," or "yeah if

I put a coat of paint on it," but all he could manage was "Would you like some tea?"

"Why—." Her eyes rolled in consideration. "—Sure."

Paul put the kettle on and got cups out while she sat at the living room table and Pete laid his math book and his tablet and his pencils out.

She sat with one ankle hooked around a chair leg—a fine figure, he thought, an artist's dream to sketch, in her form-fitting jeans. She wore mahogany loafers, a white blouse, and a white wool sweater with tiny red and blue flowers along the seams. She flipped idly through his notes. Seeing the Ufimtsev paper, she made wide eyes and her mouth opened. "Wow. Petey, honey, look at that arithmetic."

Pete groaned. "I can't figure any of that out. Why does it have a's and x's in it? Looks like the printer got all mixed up and mushed the words and the numbers together."

Paul laughed. "Yeah, well, he did, kind of, on purpose. You see, when you are a mathematician, you read mathematical notation the way lay people read text."

Marsha looked up. "I didn't realize you are a mathematician." Her eyes radiated a new respect.

"Guilty as accused. Well, to an extent, I'm really an engineer." *How to explain this?* "I was in a combined master's/doctor's program at M.I.T., and I got bored with all the theoretical stuff. I'm a hands on guy. Rockwell came along and recruited me, and I took the job. It pays well, and I get to play all day." *At least until today,* he added inwardly, morosely.

The kettle began to whistle, and Paul went into the kitchen. He turned off the gas stove and set cups and saucers on the pale yellow tiled counter. Spoons. Tea bags. Sugar.

"That's wonderful!" she gushed. She had really neat little white teeth, he noticed, and sweet lips with a touch of red lipstick. Oddly, it looked as if she'd freshly applied that lipstick, because—he dimly remembered—lipstick wore off during the course of a day. He remembered that from his mother, who'd gone to work every morning as a bookkeeper, and returned looking tired and bleary in the evenings, her lips looking pale. "Well I have big news!"

"What is it?" Paul picked up the large tray and headed into the living room.

"I got a job today at Lockheed."

"Congratulations." Paul set down the tray. She reached over, eager to help set things out. She had small, neat hands, with a little chip of rouge on each fingernail. No rings.

"I'm going to be working with various departments as an assistant auditor."

Paul frowned. "With which division is that?"

"Lockheed." She shrugged. "That's all I know. Division 243. I'm working for a Mrs. Norma Wilson. Nice lady."

Relieved not to hear any more about his friends of that morning, Paul sat down and juggled his hot teacup between his hands. He glanced down at Pete's papers.

She said: "It was going to either be Lockheed or one of the big studios. I have my degree in accounting, and I need to start working on my California CPA license, so it's a relief to know that I have steady work now."

"Can you help with this one?" Pete asked, pointing with an ink-stained finger.

Paul looked at the book. "Okay... 250 divided by 49. That 49 is almost 50, right? How many times does 50 go into 250?"

"Er..." Pete looked at his mom, who prompted him with a certain look. "Five?" he said uncertainly.

Marsha prodded: "Honey, you know that. Be sure of yourself."

"Good work," Paul said. "I see you know your multiplication tables."

Marsha said: "With an accountant for his mother, I hope so. We grilled him on the tables until he was blue in the face."

We? Paul wondered.

Paul said to Pete: "So you know the answer is somewhere around 5."

"I get it," Pete said. "49 is less than 50, so it is going to be 5. So I'll write a 5 up here. But then what do I do?"

Paul walked him through two of the problems. Then Pete started working on his own. Paul said: "I'm gonna take a peek into the back yard to see how my lawn looks. Care to join me?"

"Sure." She seemed at ease.

They walked through the kitchen, outside, across the porch, and down onto the lawn. Alberto had done a sterling job. All 25 wooden posts were exposed, each with a small dome shaped object on top.

"I saw the boy cutting the lawn," Marsha said. "I was going to ask... what are all those things?"

Paul stood with his hands in his pockets. She was a little shorter than he, maybe by three inches. "This is a little awkward. I have a security clearance, and I can't talk about my work. But I bring a little home sometimes; well, a lot of times; and this has to do with radar. I may already have said too much. I kind of fly my model airplanes over this array to do little tests. I have to ask you not to say anything to anyone."

"I promise." She looked just as awkward. "I guess this is as good a time as any, now that Peter is busy and out of earshot. I wanted you to know that he's very sensitive about his father."

The missing ring.

"My husband was a test pilot. He was killed in a crash at Nellis Air Force Base when Peter was six."

"I'm very sorry to hear that." *Ouch.*

"I'm telling you that, not to make you feel sorry for us, but so you don't say the wrong thing."

"I appreciate that."

There was a long silence.

"Mom, I'm done!"

"We'll be right in, sweetie. Check your work."

"I'll take a look at it for him."

"I don't want to put you out."

"I'm enjoying myself."

"You're very nice." She squinted into the sun, shielded her eyes a moment, then turned and regarded him directly. "I still miss him very much. I'm not ready for anything." She whirled and hurried toward the house.

Thanks for being straight with me, he wanted to say, but she fled from him. With a tinge of regret, he noted the shapeliness rear figure— not an overly skinny woman, but softly curvy without excess. The woman next door.

He followed her into the house. She already sat back in her seat, acting as if nothing had transpired, but a certain glow was gone. Paul sat down beside her son. "Let's see what you've got here, pal. First one's correct..." He checked them all. "Perfect. That was quick. Man, you must be a smart boy."

"Good genes," Marsha said.

"Good," Paul said. How to say this? How to keep the door open? "Well, you're very nice neighbors and I hope you will come over to visit more often."

She touched his arm with her fingertip, with that new colder formality. "Next time I bake a cake, you'll have to come get a piece."

"I'd like that," he said, treading his way through the hidden signals carefully. "And Pete, anytime you need help, you just come and ask."

"Can I fly your airplane again?"

"Not today, honey," she said.

"I have work to do," Paul told the boy, ruffling Pete's hair. "Maybe over the weekend."

Marsha cleaned up the tea cups, taking everything to the kitchen. In a wink, she washed the cups. "Where does the sugar go?"

"Leave it. I'll clean up."

"Thanks," she said, brushing past him, son in tow.

"Bye," Pete called out as she pulled him out the door.

Chapter 6.

The next morning, Paul knocked excitedly on Steve Rossi's office door.

"Come in!"

Paul shoved the door open. He waved the Russian paper. "Steve, I've got—." He stopped, sensing something was wrong. Steve and Ben Rich sat at the conference table, as if huddled in conversation. Their looks were serious.

"You got a haircut," Steve said.

Ben rose. He became all warmth and smiles. "How's our favorite nose cone engineer?" Without waiting for an answer he turned to Rossi. "You'll take care of your end, then?"

Steve rose. "I will."

Ben, a trim man in his 50's, with white hair and a tan, clapped Paul on the shoulder and hurried from the room. Ben was known as a tough man, but a fair one, with a brilliant mind, and many gifts from engineering through management through Federal contract politicking.

"What are you all excited about?" Steve asked Paul when they were alone.

"Look," Paul said, placing the paper on the table and forcing Steve to sit down. Both men sat. "I have a wonderful idea for a stealth technology. It's from this Russian paper."

"A Russian?" Steve asked, sitting back in sudden suspicion.

"I know what you're thinking. They're trying to throw us off the track. But they aren't. I've checked the math ten times to Sunday. Look, if they had something hot, they wouldn't let this get out, would they? I can't believe they let this paper go—it's worth gold. The Soviets missed something here, Steve, and I've caught it."

"What have you caught?"

"Diffraction. The answer isn't coatings or absorption. It's

diffraction."

"Get out."

"No, really. The numbers are all here. Old Maxwell equations are the basis. Very standard, tried and proven stuff. I need computer time, Steve. I need to run some more numbers to get the exact shape of this thing." He turned the title page over and drew a rough sketch.

"What the hell is that?" Steve asked, rumpling his upper lip.

"It's a stealthy plane."

"That thing there doesn't even look aerodynamic."

"I know. I understand. Steve, please listen. Right now it's just a concept. We have magic in our hands, and we can go someplace with it. We just need to do the testing, the R&D. We can beat any coating technology in the world."

Steve sighed. "I've known you for several years now, which is the only reason I'm not tossing you out my office door. I can get you computer time next week."

"Next week? Steve, this is hot."

"Listen to me, Paul. There's some heavy politics going on. When was the last time you took a vacation?"

Paul rose and almost yelled: "Vacation? Are you crazy? I'm on to the hottest thing we've ever done here."

Steve regarded him dourly. "Those auditors hate you. They've asked that we fire you and make room for a veteran."

"Who? What veteran?"

"Doesn't matter. Any veteran who's got the degree."

Paul sat down hard. "What?"

"You're not going to be fired, Paul. Ben and I just discussed it. He's going to bat for you. He wants you to get out of here this morning. This is a Thursday. Go home and lay low for a few days. Things will be a little different on Monday, but everything will work out okay."

"Different? How?"

"Don't know yet. The details are being worked out. Go on, Paul. Have a vacation. I'll see you Monday morning."

"But my idea—."

"Can wait. I'll listen to the whole thing next week. I'll get you twenty hours of computer time on the Big Blue, okay? We're going to take care of you, Paul, because we know what you're worth to us, even if those idiots don't."

Stunned, Paul marched down the corridor and to his car, which was parked in a reserved space nose-in to the building, at the end of the same row that started with Kelly Johnson, then Ben Rich, then Steve Rossi, and so on down the line. Paul was the most junior senior engineer. Paul tossed the paper in the trunk of his car—noticing the library books there—and peeled out. He drove to the gate so fast the guard came out and told him to slow down. He was boiling.

Chapter 7.

As he drove to Madeira, Paul kept thinking over and over again, the Sixties are over... for everyone except those fossils.

He pulled up at the library and got the books from the trunk. For the second day in a row, he was experiencing what it was like to not be at work, and it was a strange feeling. Where he should have felt elated at using well-earned vacation time, he instead felt butterflies in his stomach. The lovely sunshine, the cloudless skies, the smells of mown grass and blooming flowers, all should have made him feel happy. Instead, he felt kind of sick inside. His world was being wrenched apart. His life was being turned upside down, all because of a couple of dim old bureaucrats.

The library was one of his favorite places. He should come here more often—but who had time? It smelled of paper and bindings inside. It was a small library, but it was darkish and had cozy nooks where people sat and read.

Wanda Burley was a heavyset middle-aged woman who evidently was trying to keep her hair the same shade of carrot red it had been when she was young in the '50's. A pleasant, attractive woman, she had telltale wisps of white around her ears, and a pair of reading glasses hung on her white blouse front. "Mr. Owens! My gosh, I almost forgot what you look like."

"I'm sorry, Mrs. Burley." He put the four books in a stack before her. "I've just been so busy..."

"I understand." She looked distressed. "Mr. Owens, I'm afraid to check what the fines will be."

"It's okay, Mrs. Burley. I deserve it." He took out his checkbook. Lay it on me. I have courage."

"Okay." She put a sheet of microfiche in the reader and frowned.

"Couple of men here asking questions about you yesterday."

"Oh?" His stomach butterflied again. It was an unfamiliar feeling, but he was beginning to think it would be a regular part of his life from now on.

"Twelve fifty," she mumbled, writing the number on a slip of scrap paper. "I will only fine you one half of the purchase price of each book. Since they are relatively old books, this won't clean you out, but I imagine it will hurt." She searched for the price of the second book. "They said they're FBI. Wanted to know if you come here a lot. What kind of books you read. Got me all upset. And hot under the collar. You'd think it was Russia here or something."

Paul stammered: "What did they say? Why are they doing this?"

"Hmph! 'Just a routine background check,' they said."

Paul bit his lip. He'd already had a complete check and carried a Top Secret clearance. If anything happened for him to get bumped down, or to lose that entirely, he'd never be able to work in a Government facility again.

"Twenty four dollars and ten cents," Mrs. Burley pronounced. "You can pay me five bucks a month, how's that?"

"No, no. I'll write you a check for the whole amount."

`As he wrote, she pulled out a typewritten list. "I had to show them this. I had to get this list together for the Central Library because of your way overdue books." She laid the list in front of him and pointed at one item with a red pencil mark beside it. It said *Progressive Forces in the Soviet Union, Connerly, Harvard University Press, 1969.* "They made a photocopy of this list. That's their check mark."

He guffawed. "My God—I spotted something in passing in that book and took it home to read about three paragraphs about how they treat scientists at Moscow University."

"Hoover's boys at work," she said with a shrug. "I feel safe now."

He paid her and left the library without bothering to browse.

He didn't have the stomach for it. Sweat ran down his face, down his back. He felt like driving back to the plant and shaking Steve Rossi's lapels. This was a bad dream—a sudden nightmare. It couldn't be happening. He'd been so happy the past few years, so utterly secure with his toys and his nose cones.

He understood now. He wasn't on vacation time. He was suspended while these auditors ran an FBI investigation on him. He cringed suddenly when he realized that Marsha had just begun work there. Would she know about this? Only a matter of time, he thought grimly as he drove home.

Chapter 8.

Paul came to a screeching stop in his driveway.

He got out of the car. As he raised the old garage door, it made a shudder and a crash.

He flicked on the lights.

His canoe, his bicycle, his skis sat there gathering dust.

He pulled the 23-pound aluminum racing bicycle out and slammed the door shut.

In the house, he got a glass of water. He nearly felt faint and had to steady himself at the kitchen sink. He changed into a T-shirt and shorts. Slipped into his tennis shoes. Dug his helmet out of the hall closet on his way out.

He swung onto the bicycle and began pedaling furiously, letting his anger out on the machine. The road gritted under his tires like broken glass, like snarling teeth. He clenched his jaws and leaned over the curved handlebars, pumping uphill in first gear, pumping in 7th gear on flat stretches.

Pretty soon, he was far from home, far from the plant, far from his troubles.

Sweaty and tired, he slowed to a steady pace. The work of bicycling took over from the work of being scared, of being angry, of having butterflies. The anxiety was still there but it was more abstract than the cramp in his right calf, the aching of his gluteal muscles, the redness and pulpiness of his palms as they gripped the sticky electrical tape wrapped around the handlebars. He began to puff a bit—out of shape!

At last, he stopped for a cola in a strip mall.

Then he turned back home. Pumping, pumping...

Hypnotized with fatigue, he rolled into the driveway, kicked the bike aside, tossed his helmet off with both hands, and threw himself on his back on the lawn. Gasping for air, he rolled around, trying to stop panting. He wound up on all fours, sucking oxygen through abraded lips scoured by hours of cycling in the desert air.

God, this was crazy.

Slowly, he limped into the house.

He took a long, hot shower, then soaked in the hot water left over.

Finally, toweling himself off, he went into the kitchen to get a beer.

Pete's voice piped in the doorway. "Mr. Owens!"

Paul nearly dropped his towel.

Pete's shadow was glued to the screen, his nose and fingertips pink. "Mr. Owens?"

"Hi, Pete. Gimme a minute."

"Okay."

Paul dressed quickly and went to the door toweling his hair. "How are you?"

"I'm fine. Can I come in?"

"Sure." Paul pushed the door open.

Pete came in, his blue eyes serious, his hands in his pockets. "Are you going to fly model airplanes today?"

"Uh—well, I wasn't planning on it."

Pete stared at him stolidly, and Paul began to think there had to be something more than suffering from this anxiety. "You wanna fly the plane awhile?"

Pete grinned and waved his fist. "Yeah!"

"Okay, come on."

Paul sat on the porch, while the boy ran around the yard, and the white wings of Condor I dipped this way and that.

"Nice job of fixing it," Pete said.

"Thanks. It wasn't much. Lucky you didn't sit on it or anything."

"Yeah. That would have been a shame. She's a beauty."

Paul thought about the boy's father. What could he say? Marsha had made it clear he must watch every word. Should he ask: "do you like planes a lot?" or "wanna be a pilot?" No, it was best to remain silent. Let the kid enjoy himself.

Round and round Condor went over the radar array. Up. Down. Left. Right. Yaw. Roll. Pitch.

The stealth design would have to be on all sides. Diamond shapes that threw off radar signals the way a diamond threw off sparkling wheels of light. In fact, this object, if it should ever fly, would have to be faceted like a diamond, with thousands of flat triangular shapes, none of which would have a radar cross-section greater than the point of a pin. To prove that, he'd have to build a model. Damn it! He wished he were at the plant so he could start right away. Typically, he'd spent the next few weeks practically living in his laboratory, working day and night, sending out for sandwiches and milk.

But maybe this was a godsend.

He smiled at the little 9 year old boy innocently hopping around.

Condor swooped down and looped between several posts before soaring high again. Paul clapped. "Hey, that was great!"

Someone else clapped and whistled. Marsha, watching from her kitchen window.

A minute later she came outside, wearing a long fine cotton print dress in warm russets and yellows, that outlined the fine contours of her slim figure as she walked and as the wind blew around her. Her smile sparkled, and Paul was captivated. He felt a little sad, because he understood her loss. He understood that he had no chance with her, and he let that thought go away as if he were releasing a helium balloon.

"Peter, you be careful with that plane."

"Okay, Mom!" Pete piped without looking at her. He chased Condor's snow-white tail.

"How are you?" she asked, standing near him with her hands clasped behind her back. Her expression was complex and unreadable—but pleasant and companionable.

"I've had better days."

"That bad, huh?"

"Thanks to that new batch of auditors."

"Oh, the old Navy chiefs?" She laughed. "They are a regulation crew if I ever saw one."

"Have you met Alex Fitch yet?"

She shook her head lightly. Nothing registered in her eyes, so he knew she had not met Fitch yet. He did not have a good feeling about any of them, but especially Fitch.

"I'm going away for the weekend," he said. The plan was forming in his head as he spoke. "I want to get away from it all for a few days. I'm wondering if you can watch the store for me. You know, just look in on the house now and then."

"I'll be happy to."

Condor flew over Marsha's head as Pete came running. "Where are you going to?"

Paul thought for a second. "San Diego, I think. I'll just drive down there and do a little surfing."

"I'd like to learn how to surf."

"Peter!"

"I'm a good swimmer. My dad taught me how to swim."

The two adults remained carefully silent. Pete ran to catch Condor before it could crash. The engine conked out—no more fuel—and landed in his arms.

"Well done," Paul said.

Pete came running and handed the plane and the controls over. "Will you take me surfing some time?"

"Sure. If your mom says it's okay."

"Can we go to San Diego with you?"

Paul laughed and Marsha gasped.

"I'm serious. I've always wanted to go surfing, and I hear it's real great at Solana Beach. You know the Beach Boys song?" Pete swiveled his hips and snapped his fingers as if the Beach Boys' music were playing. "Surfing U.S.A. Down in La Jolla, and Waiamea too. Bushy bushy blond surfing, surfing U.S.A.!"

"Wow," Paul said, "a pop singer too."

"I'm sorry," Marsha said, "we're going to be busy this weekend, and I'm sorry my son is—."

"We are not, Mom," Pete said. "We are just going to hang around and be bored, like we are every weekend."

"Don't argue with me, Peter."

"I'm not, I'm just saying—"

"It would be fine with me," Paul said, not nearly half seriously.

"I wanna go!" Pete yelled.

"Peter!"

"He said we could."

"I'm sorry," Paul said. "Me and my big mouth."

"I'll think about it."

"Thanks, Mom!"

"Peter!"

Paul handed the plane back to the boy. "See if you can fly it to the ravine and back."

"Okay!" Pete and the plane sped away.

Paul told her: "I understand your situation. Look, we're neighbors and we're friends. I need a short vacation, and if you'd like to get away, you're welcome."

"How would we fit into your Mustang? Or my little car?"

"I'm planning to borrow a friend's VW bus. It has a pop-up camper on top. You and Pete could sleep in that, and I'll just pitch my pup tent alongside."

"Absolutely not. That would be inconveniencing you."

"I could really use the company," he said. "The friendship would far outweigh a little inconvenience."

She looked at him for a long minute. "Okay." She shrugged. "Okay," she repeated seeming to like the idea. She nodded to herself, smiling.

Paul extended a hand, and she shook. "Plato will go with us," he promised, and he meant it.

That evening, Paul stayed up late at the dining room table with catalogs, a pad, pencils, a drawing kit including compass and protractor, a slide rule, his calculator, and a T-square. He knew what he must do. On Monday, he would have to hit the deck running. He must have a plan, and this would be it: He would build a small model of his plane. It would not be enough to convince Steve and Ben that the concept worked on paper. He would build a small mockup. He could not possibly duplicate in cardboard the thousands of tiny triangular facets needed, but if the model could even diminish the signature by 25% he'd be doing better than most of the absorption composites.

He hardly noticed that the lights winked out, one by one, next door.

Chapter 9.

On Friday, Paul rose at daybreak, wolfed down a couple of egg salad sandwiches with milk, and raced out the door. Marsha and Pete weren't up yet, for her kitchen light was dark.

Paul drove down into Burbank, and from there into Los Angeles. He had his checkbook in his rear pocket, and several catalogs on the Mustang's passenger seat.

There was a thick layer of smog over the city. The air hurt to breathe, and Paul's eyes grew teary. An ugly brown cloud hung over the city, like a twisted rope made by a giant. It glowed coppery-yellow in places where the sunlight hit it, and loomed darkly in shades of brown and black where the light was blocked.

One by one he entered the leading hobby shops.

His first question, which he asked an elderly black man who stood behind the counter of Kalsom's Hobbies in Hollywood: "What's the best hovering machine available?"

The man twisted his lips in bemusement. "What do you want to hover for?"

"It's a top secret U.S. government project."

"Ha ha ha ha!" the man laughed out loud. "That's a good one!"

"Just kidding," Paul said. "I want something very stable that will stand still. It's got to be strong enough to lift, say, a pound. And it needs to have enough fuel capacity for at least five minutes of flight time."

"Hmm. That's getting into big time." He pointed at the models hanging from the ceiling. "Ever think about using a small blimp?"

Paul stared at the lovely dark blue sausage shape, about 16 feet long. "How much?"

"Thousand dollars."

"Ooops. I was thinking more like $250."

The man shook his head. "You can get away with a helicopter of some kind, maybe $500, if you buy parts and assemble your own. A kit, maybe. I don't carry them. But I can tell you who does."

Ouch! Paul had money in the bank, and he earned good money, but he had a mortgage to pay, and owning a Mustang wasn't so cheap.

One by one, he explored the various hobby haunts around L.A., and by the time he headed home to Madeira, he had the parts he needed.

On the way, he stopped and traded cars with an old girlfriend, Marie, whom he'd actually lived with for a year or so in his early days at Lockheed. She was a cute, freckled blonde, and they kept in touch. They exchanged a little conversation, swapped keys, and kissed goodbye. Paul carried his boxes to the van, got in, and drove off.

Chapter 10.

"Ready?"

Marsha stood at the front door, Pete by her side. She wore a flowered dress, cute little light-blue canvas deck shoes, a straw hat, and sunglasses. She smiled with excitement.

Pete wore a Hawaiian shirt in reds, blue shorts, and sandals. Sunglasses hung by a cord around his neck, and he wore a Lockheed baseball cap. He lugged a huge sack of plastic water toys. A row of suitcases and a cooler and several hand grips sat on the lawn by the van.

"Good morning," Paul answered. "Give me a minute to lock up the house."

Minutes later, they were on their way down into L.A. and from there on the 405 Freeway to the 5 down through Orange County into San Diego.

On the way down, Marsha and Paul chattered about their lives and ambitions, what they enjoyed and didn't enjoy, movies they planned to see. Pete sat on the rear half-seat, playing with toy cars. He sat turned away and concentrated on his game.

Marsha was from Salem, Oregon. Her parents were retired school teachers. ("No wonder Pete inherited all those smarts!" Paul said). Marsha Smith had met Jeffrey Kassner when they were in college together at Oregon State. Jeffrey had been in Air Force ROTC and had served as a pilot at Travis AFB and later Nellis. At Nellis, he'd resigned his commission to become a civilian test pilot. He'd been killed in the crash of an experimental version of the F-4 Phantom. She showed Paul a picture of Jeffrey—he'd been a slim, handsome man with neatly combed blond hair and an expression of complete, quiet self-confidence. "We had it all," Marsha said quietly, so Pete wouldn't hear.

Paul, keeping both hands on the wheel, nodded at the photo and she put it away. He said: "I wish it had turned out differently."

"Thanks." It was clear she wished it too. She sat back and put one bare foot up against the dashboard. "Let's enjoy our weekend."

They tooled down I-5 through Anaheim, where Disneyland was, then through Santa Ana and Oceanside, and by one they were in Solana Beach. They had lunch in a restaurant whose patio overlooked rough surf in which dolphins and seals played, nearly on the beach. Pete gaped, pointing at every marvel. Paul had been here before, and it was a little bit old hat, but still very nice. He was happy for her that Marsha appeared to be enjoying herself. She looked about, her sunglasses reflecting glare, and grinned. "You can really smell the sea here." She coated her face, and Pete's, with sunscreen. "You should really use this too," she told Paul. Sliding closer with her chair, she dabbed little swaths of milky looking cream on Paul's cheeks. Her fingers were gentle but thorough. The smell reminded him of her: clean, lightly coconut, enticing. "Thanks," he told her when she was done. He paid the bill, and they headed down to the water. They carried towels, a small cooler, aluminum tubular-framed chairs to sit in, and two surf boards. One was Paul's; the other had the initials JMK on one end in permanent marker. Paul wondered if Jeffrey's middle name had been Mike or Mark or something. He felt kind of like an intruder, and promised himself to be respectful of her feelings and her space.

There were puffy white clouds on the distant western horizon, far out at sea, and a storm was coming in the next day or two. Marsha, who wore a burgundy two-piece bikini, did not like swimming that much. Paul watched her surreptitiously, liking her. She preferred to wade in the water, letting the four foot swells from the storm rise and fall around her, timing it so that she was in the exact middle of where each wave peaked. Several other men and women were doing the same. The more adventurous, wearing wetsuits, paddled into the tide.

Paul took Pete out a hundred feet or so while Marsha watched anxiously. No need—the water was only about six feet deep here, and the boy was an excellent swimmer, a natural. Paul held the board while Pete climbed onto it and tried so stand. He kept falling down, and this climbing and falling must have taken a half hour before just the right wave came, at just the right moment, and Pete found his sea legs just then. Off he went, flying to the left and right, before falling off. "Good work!" Paul hollered as Pete paddled back. "I think you went thirty feet on your first try. That's darn good."

"It is? Hey, thanks!"

Marsha made her way out, paddling lightly. "How are you guys doing?"

"Just fine," Pete yelled. "Hey mom, watch me surf the wild waves! Help me up, Mr. Owens. Here I go. Whoo-pee!" He caught a wave and sailed along with it, gradually losing his balance, until he fell backward into the water. He emerged splashing and blowing bubbles, yelling "Cool! Did you see that? Man this is great."

"He's having a blast," Marsha said. "Thanks for bringing us along."

"My pleasure."

Later in the afternoon, they rinsed off at public showers, and then took turns changing in the van. It got cold, and they shivered with goose bumps. Each wore jeans and a thick sweater. Marsha's lips were blue, and Paul put his arm around her. "Let's go get some hot tea!"

"Ggg," she said, and slipped an eel-cold arm around him, making him yelp.

"God you're cold," he said.

"Cold hands, warm heart." She hugged him tightly. He put his other arm around Pete, and together they walked down to the same place they'd had lunch. Darkness fell, and they sat together sipping coffee. Pete walked out on the patio and stood leaning on the wooden railing, watching the sky full of stars above, and lights moving across the Pacific Ocean below.

It was kind of a magic moment, Paul thought. He sat very close beside Marsha in plush beige leather furniture. They were tired from the water. He could have put his arm around her, but he didn't. He was pretty sure she'd let him, but he thought it was enough to sit with her. She sighed dreamily and leaned her head lightly against his shoulder. "I'm hungry, but I can't move."

"Let's order something light," he suggested.

They decided on fish and chips, which wasn't so light, but there wasn't too much to the single order they shared. She wasn't a big eater, so Pete and Paul nearly split the meal. "It's dark, and I'm not up for finding a camp ground at this hour. Let's do it in the morning."

"Oh, Paul! I think it would be wonderful to camp here by the ocean!"

They drove the camper as close as they could to the beach. They sat on the sea wall for a good two hours, chatting with other couples, while Pete found a few local kids to chase around with. Paul and Marsha kept a wary eye on Pete's silhouette as he scampered around the water line. Somebody's large, shaggy old house dog joined the kids in a game of tag, and the dog seemed to know the rules.

"It's nice here," Marsha said dreamily.

"More exciting than Burbank?"

"Reminds me of Oregon. The beaches there are beautiful."

"More beautiful than here?"

"Yes."

"You gonna move back there someday?"

"I dunno. My parents are still around, and I have a brother and sister. The only reason I ever left, really, was because of Jeffrey."

Paul didn't know quite what to say, and so he watched Pete disinterestedly. Suddenly he realized she was sobbing. She held her knuckles to her mouth, and big tear drops squeezed out of her closed eyes. Instinctively, he put his arm around her, but she turned and walked several arms' lengths away.

She stopped crying after a few minutes. Paul handed her a napkin that he'd put in his pocket in the restaurant and then forgotten. "Thank you," she said, and walked away down to the water. "I'm sorry," she whispered over her shoulder. She picked up a Frisbee and ran lightly, throwing it to her son, but he dog caught it and ran down the beach. The dark silhouettes chased the dog and ran out of sight.

Paul waited, leaning on the railing. *I'm lucky,* he thought. I'm alive, and I don't have her problems. Okay, so if I lose the job, I can go back to college and finish my Ph.D. I can always teach. In the same mental breath, he realized how much he'd miss the hands-on work. And, frankly, the secrecy and the urgency were like aphrodisiacs.

Marsha and Pete came up the sand after a while. "I am so tired," she said. Pete was fairly staggering. She put her arm around Paul's and tugged him powerfully along, squeezing his arm against her side. "Let's put this boy to bed. We all going to crash in the van?"

"It's the only solution," Paul said. "I'm too beat."

"Well, you do what's right. I trust you to know the answers."

The ocean breeze was mild, and there was a tang of eucalyptus in the air. It was already quiet along the water. Marsh climbed in back with Pete and spread out his sleeping bag. "I'm going to find us a quieter, darker, safer spot," Paul said. Starting the van, he swung the VW around and trundled up the street with chattering engine. A few streets up and to one side, they came to a residential neighborhood dark with tree crowns. Paul pulled up at the curb, locked all the doors, and pulled curtains on all the windows. He unbolted the popup and pushed it open. The wedge-shaped lid, with plastic accordion sides, locked into place, leaving a shallow space at the rear, tapering quickly to about three feet clearance toward the front.

In the faint dome light, she bent over her son, zipping his bag shut. "He's out cold," she murmured. "I won't be far behind."

"Me neither," Paul said. "I'll sit with you for a few minutes, and then I'll climb up top." He pictured himself pushing the hatch open, climbing up with his sleeping bag, closing the hatch, and crawling into the bag to fade instantly.

With Pete asleep against the far side, and Marsha in the middle, Paul lay on his bag near the sealed sliding door. He turned the dome light out.

In the dark, they listened to a distant ship's horn. A wind blew lightly around the van, nudging it as if someone were pushing a pinkie finger against it—very lightly. Frequently, pine needles or other debris fell on the roof with a faint plop noise. At first Marsha jumped, but he reassured her, and they laughed.

They lay side by side, listening to each other breathe.

"I'm sorry about back there."

"What?"

"Crying."

"Don't be."

"I'm not ready to move on yet, Paul. You're a very nice man, but I'm not even ready to think of you as anything more than a nice friend and neighbor. Can you understand that?"

"I've never had a spouse die on me, so I can only imagine that it's very terrible."

"You're very honest, and quite understanding."

"This is a great trip, don't you think?"

"It's the nicest thing I've done in quite a while. Pete adores you."

"He's a slick little guy. I'm going to be building a new plane in the next few weeks, and he can help me test fly it."

"He talks a lot about you, Paul. I hope he's not a burden to you."

"Not a bit. He's company. I live alone."

"Oh yes. I've forgotten what that's like. Are you okay?"

"I work so many hours that I guess I'm okay. I keep busy."

"Any girlfriends? Am I being too nosy?"

"Nah. Nobody right now. Actually, this van belongs to an ex-girlfriend that I lived with for a year. We're still good friends."

They lay on their backs, looking up, and Paul stared up through a slit between the curtain and the window. A tree branch waved hypnotically over a field of stars. He heard Marsha snoring lightly. Her breath felt cool against his cheek, and he smelled again that faint fresh-coconut lotion. Then sleep overcame him.

Paul awoke to the sound of Pete yelling. "Mom! I'm hungry and I have a headache!"

Paul opened his eyes and looked into the face of Marsha, who lay facing him, studying him as if he were a complex painting. She was so close he could have stretched his neck slightly to kiss her. She put her hand over her mouth and turned away, whispering "I have morning breath."

Groaning, Paul sat up, rubbing his neck. He had only the floor rug for a pad, and his muscles were stiff.

Marsha started feeding Pete milk and crackers with cheese from the cooler. "He says he had bad dreams last night." She leaned close and muttered: "He still has nightmares about his dad crashing and burning." Then: "He gets these headaches and he has to eat or he'll be achy and grouchy all day."

Pete said: "What are we going to do today, Mr. Owens?"

Paul said: "Well, it's Sunday. It's early—seven a.m. We'll make another long day of it. We'll drive over to Palomar Mountain and go biking, how's that?"

"Sounds adventuresome, Paul."

"It's not quite like climbing Mt. Everest, but it will do."

"Didn't realize you're such an outdoorsman." She squeezed his bicep.

Paul told Pete: "Ever been to the 200 inch telescope there, the Hale?"

Pete made wide eyes.

"It can look farther into space than any other instrument ever made by man."

"How far?"

"So many miles that you couldn't write all the zeroes on a sheet of paper."

"Wow! Can we look at some stars?"

"Well, not in the daytime. But they have a museum."

"Sounds like fun," Marsha said, dishing out a makeshift breakfast.

It was a pleasant drive inland, through meandering orange groves filled with millions of fruit as if someone had gone crazy putting cloth dots on a greenboard. They tooled around and around the sides of Palomar Mountain, until they came to a fork about a mile up. "To the left is a state park," Paul said, "and straight ahead is the observatory."

He pulled ahead a few yards and swung into a parking lot on the left. "There's a little hippie store here, and a restaurant, and one or two other things. We can wash up a bit and get something warm to eat."

As they walked across the parking lot, Marsha said: "I'm still stiff from all that activity yesterday."

Later, as Paul drove further into the densely wooded summit, the huge dome of the Hale loomed over the treetops.

"It's like science fiction," Marsha said, gaping.

"Wow!" Pete said, "I'll bet they can see a bug on the moon, if there were life there, which there isn't, right, Mr. Owens?"

"Right."

They bicycled around the summit for a while, getting a little short of breath at the crisp air and high altitude. It was colder up here, Paul noted, and the air was cleaner.

"Man, we're all going to sleep like rocks again tonight," Marsha said laughing as she wobbled along one of the dirt trails.

"Good for you!"

Pete found some kids to run around with. Paul and Marsha sat on a huge granite boulder overlooking the parking lot, in a grove of gigantic ancient cedars of Lebanon. "If only life were always like this," she said.

"We wouldn't enjoy it then."

"You're always so philosophical."

"I'm sorry."

"No, I like it. You can think clearly. You can see a situation and know what to do, how to act. It's a great quality." She gave him a troubled look. "Are you sure I'm not a nuisance? I'm carrying all this weight on my back, this baggage—."

"You can start crying again if you'd like."

"—About this man I loved so much—."

Paul reached out to put his arm around her, remembering how she'd run away last night. What else could he do? "Maybe you need to cry more often."

Tears filled her eyes. "I'm not going to cry this time."

"Maybe crying is good for the soul."

Tears streamed down her face. "I'm not going to cry. I'm going to sit here and just behave myself." She pulled out the same napkin—now shredded—that he'd given her last night. "I'm really sorry, Paul. I wish I weren't putting you through this."

"Through what?"

She dabbed one eye, then the other. "I don't know if I can ever get it together again. I'm thirty years old, and I've been a widow since I was 27. I don't think I can ever love another man, and that's why I just want to be friends. I don't know what Peter would do if he saw me kissing a man or whatever, and I'm sorry we keep having this stupid conversation."

He pulled his arm back. "It's okay, Marsha. I'm having a really hard time at work right now, and I wish I could cry about it. Men just don't cry that easily. I envy you."

"I'm being very selfish." She held her hand over her mouth, horrified.

"No, you're not. You're taking my mind off my troubles by sharing your troubles, which are much more important than mine."

She slid close and put her arm tightly around his shoulders, pulling him close. She stroked his hair with her free hand and said: "I'm willing to listen to your troubles if you want to share them."

He laughed. "The first problem is that my troubles are so top secret that I could go to jail if I tell anyone, and I might take you with me."

They shared a loud laugh, and she still held him, when Pete appeared in the distance. He looked like an animal caught in the headlights.

"Oh no," Marsha said, pulling away.

Pete turned and ran into the forest.

She pulled her feet close and wrapped her arms around her shirt, around her legs. "Oh dear. I wonder how he's going to react now. Maybe he'll punish me. Sometimes he does that because somehow he's mad at me that Jeffrey died." She paused. "Jesus, there I go again. Any man I have a relationship with will have to share me with Jeffrey. It's not fair. I'm never going to get involved again."

Paul cleared his throat. "Well, never is a long time."

She picked at the little woodsy debris and dust by her thigh. "I knew when I fell in love with him that he liked to take risks. He was a sober, good man. Never hit me, never yelled at me, even when I was pregnant and forgetful and kept losing my car keys and my car or running out of gas and dropping things. After Peter grows up, if I ever get involved in a relationship again, I won't do it with a risk taker. I would want a steady, safe man, someone with a secure career, who can provide for us, and who's not going to crash and die. I think you need a more adventuresome woman, Paul."

"Well, I'm not proposing to you."

"I'm sorry."

"I'm just your neighbor. I find you very attractive, but right now everything is wide open, so maybe you'll take another trip like this someday with me, and that's about as far as we have to think ahead, okay?"

"Okay."

The trip back down the mountain was slow and tedious, and the three of them didn't talk much. They sat comfortably in one another's presence and stared at the passing scenery. Darkness fell, and ships' lights appeared on the Pacific as they drove north on I-5. Around 9 p.m., they pulled up at their homes in Madeira. The stars made a twinkling canopy overhead. Paul carried a sleeping Pete into Marsha's house—it was cute inside, feminine without being overly frilly, but very tidy. She ran ahead into a smaller bedroom that was covered posters and toys and stuffed animals. She pulled the covers back, and Paul laid the boy on his side, where he snored. "I have to change him into the jammies," she said. She slipped her arm through his. "Come on, I'll walk you home."

When they were outside, she locked the door, then took Paul's arm. He felt the curve of her waist against his elbow, like the rhythm in a poem, and the sharpness of her hip bone. "We should take walks some evenings," she said.

"I'd like that—when I'm not buried in my work."

"I hope all goes well with the job."

"I hope so too."

They came to his little front porch.

She took his hands in hers. "Paul, we had a wonderful time."

"I'm glad." He wanted to take her in his arms, but pushed the idea away.

"You're going to meet someone nice with no complications that's going to be just perfect for you. In the meantime, I do believe that a wonderful date like this deserves a kiss for both participants." She fidgeted awkwardly. "Well, I mean, it's like a custom, right?"

He took her to him, marveling at how well she folded into his embrace, and how soft she felt against his body. He put his hand behind her head and gently tilted it so he could approach her lips with his. He felt her hands rise up his back and cup the back of his head as he encountered the nervous dryness of her mouth. In a moment, their tongues were intertwined, and they kissed in hungry gulps. Weakly, he leaned back against a porch pillar as they continued their starved kissing. Finally, she pulled back. "If I don't run now, Paul, we'll both regret it." She touched his cheek lightly in passing and then sprinted away into the dark. Dazed, he listened as she fumbled with her key. "Good night!" she said.

"Good night." It was all he could say.

Chapter 11.

When Paul arrived at work, he found a security guard hovering around the parking area. Paul drove right into his old parking spot, only to hear the guard yelling and to notice that there was a new sign up: "Reserved. Alex Fitch."

The guard approached the rolled down window. "I'm sorry, Paul. They switched everything around. Wait until you get inside. You won't recognize the place."

"Thanks." Paul backed up and found a spot several rows away. Grabbing his Ufimtsev paper, he walked toward the plant.

As he walked down the long, shadowy corridor, whose ancient linoleum sparkled like some underwater glass, he spotted Steve Rossi down the hall. Rossi, wearing a dark suit, white tie, and dark red tie, stood half in and half out of his office. When he saw Paul, he started walking.

Paul pushed the door of his lab open—and froze.

Everything was gone. Along one wall were a group of cardboard boxes—Alex Fitch's?—and some ugly gray metal filing cabinets.

Paul felt as if there were a hole at the bottom of his stomach, and sand were running out.

"Paul."

"What the hell happened?"

"We're moving things around. Come into my office and don't say anything until I get the door closed."

Paul followed as in a dream. He sat down in Steve's narrow, cluttered office. Pictures on the wall showed rockets lifting off, with employees' signatures on them; planes the Skunk Works had built; awards Steve had won.

Steve closed the door. "I'm sorry, Paul. None of this was our idea.

You know that Ben and Kelly and I support you 100%."

Paul said leadenly: "The FBI has been questioning people about me. It's embarrassing."

Steve sat at his desk and winced.

"I'm embarrassed that the librarian had to give them a list of what I read. What are they going to say when they find out I've been reading a Soviet mathematical paper?" Paul shook the Ufimtsev paper, his fist trembling with rage. "That I'm a Communist spy? If I can't get you to listen to me, what can I expect from these auditors and the FBI?"

"I don't blame you for being angry. I'm angry too, Paul. Do you know what we're up against here? There are vast sums in contracts floating around. I just found out we may have missed getting a million bucks of seed money for a proof of concept on a new class of stealth planes. So what the Government does, because contractors have a reputation of cost overruns and inefficiency, is they put pressure on companies. And, hey, we're the Skunk Works, we're one of the loosest organizations around. When those guys came in here, it was like a den of iniquity to them. They are going to be doing—as far as Ben and Kelly can stop them—what they do at all the other big contractors— General Dynamics, Northrop, you name it. They'll send auditors in unannounced to inspect people's cubicles. No photos, no cartoons, no jokes, no nothing. Bare walls. Clean, bare desk with all work neatly put in drawers. Christ, Paul, they don't even treat active military like this, but it's that 1940's mentality. They're military men from the old school." He paused to light a cigarette. "And then there's you." He puffed. "One look at you and the Sixties came alive again. I've got news for you. Those guys weren't under fire in any foxholes. Most of them were Navy and Army NCOs pushing paperwork. That's why they're here. They know paperwork. They know bureaucracy. They are from Byzantium, and they invented petty intrigue. And, unfortunately, they hate your guts on sight, no questions asked. What small minds they have are already made up."

"Am I fired?"

"Fired? No. But you're damaged. There is only so much we can do. If it makes you feel a little better, Kelly and Ben are talking to a four-star Air Force officer about this."

"What about 'this' exactly, anyway, Steve?"

" 'This,' as you call it, is that they're throwing everything at you that they can. Including the FBI. You're gonna come out clean like you did before, because you have a Top Secret clearance now, so why should anything be any different?"

"They'll find something."

"Didn't last time."

"They will invent something if they have to."

"Now wait a minute, Paul. Not the FBI. Don't accuse them of—."

"Okay. Maybe I'm overreacting if that is possible. Where is all my stuff?"

"It's under lock and key."

"My private property."

"It's in a temporary hold status, Paul."

Paul rose and leaned against the wall. He leaned his forearm against the wall and stared at the fist he was making. He felt rage rushing in his ears.

"Paul take it easy."

Paul took a deep breath, wound up, and slammed his fist down on Steve's little side table so hard that the metal bent a little. Then he realized he'd lashed out at a friend and sat down. He covered his face in shame. "I'm sorry."

"No problem," Steve said, grunting as he tried to straighten the little metal drawer.

Paul rose, put his knee against it, straightened it, and pushed it into the desk. "That was uncalled for and I apologize."

"Just so you don't hit me like that. I'm too out of shape."

"I've never hit anyone in my life."

"Good." Steve sat upright and raised both palms. "Paul, you have a little bit of a temper, and I want to warn you—don't play into the hands of these dickheads. Be cool."

"Okay, I'm cool. Where's my crap?"

"Under lock and key while the FBI check is going on. They have to check through all your gear because you're under this investigation. And now the bad news."

"Oh Christ, now what?"

"Your clearance is temporarily dropped from Top Secret to Secret until the results are back. Which could take a few weeks, or even months."

"Oh no."

"And that means I can't let you on the shop floor. I have to replace you until we can get your TS back. I'm sorry."

"I can't believe this. We haven't even discussed what's in this paper." He waved the paper again.

"You got my ear."

Paul was almost too upset to talk, so he blurted it out in chunks he hoped were not too incoherent. "Not coatings alone. Not absorption by itself. Shape, structure, and absorption. I think we can get at least a tenfold reduction in the back signature, but I won't know for sure until I can test. I can't test until I get a model built. I can't get a model built until I draw up the designs. And I can't do that until I get approval from you."

Steve looked almost happy. "Will that keep you busy?"

"Yeah. Will you help me?"

"You bet. We don't want to lose you, Paul. You're one of the best there is. We just have to sweat this out. If they don't find anything more than they didn't find last time around, we could be back in business in a month or so. They're just throwing their weight around anyway they can, and you're an easy target. They have our attention now, see, and that's what they're really after."

"Bastards."

"Yeah, they are. What do we know? Maybe they have to be. Aw hell, Paul, I'm sorry about all this and I'll do everything I can to help you. There is an office available in a non TS work area if you want, or you can work from home."

"Okay." A little of the glow returned to Paul. "Listen, I'll explain this whole concept to you. Since it's not an official project, you can help me without getting in trouble. I'm going to work from home as much as I can—."

"—Good. Keep a low profile—."

"—Right. And I'm going to have you build a small prototype for me. Now the first thing I'll need is computer time."

"How much?"

"Fifty hours of CPU time."

"Whew. That's a lot. I think we can sneak you in between batch jobs at night. It'll be disjointed—twenty minutes here, thirty minutes there."

"That will have to do. I'm going to go home and work on the equations. I'll need to write some FORTRAN programs. But now, let me explain what I think we have here." He rose and stepped to the small blackboard. Picking up a piece of chalk, he drew a triangle while Steve listened intently. "As long as this figure is not perpendicular to you, and it's coated with Radar Absorbent Material (RAM), and it has the latest inner layered absorption structures and materials, this shape will send you almost a zero return." Bit by bit, he led Steve, who had a decent grasp of mathematics from a practical engineering standpoint, into the new world of stealth that he could envision so clearly by now. And Steve began to nod appreciatively. "The only thing is the aerodynamics obviously suck, so it's going to be a hard sell. But I'll hear you out, and I'm sure Ben will too. Just don't get your hopes up.

Remember, we're trying to buy you a low profile? Everyone believes in absorption. If you try to run the ball another way on the court, you'll be noticed."

Chapter 12.

Paul's new temporary office was a small, unattractive one in a building off Mahogany Row. Paul's heart sank when he explored it, but he realized that he had a purpose to accomplish.

As he stared at the bare walls—off-baby blue scarred with old tape marks, pencil streaks, laundry marker graffiti—and the brown linoleum floor that was missing a few tiles, he realized how precarious his position was. Nobody had said this to him yet, but he knew that he must be able to prove his new technology.

He had a battered wooden desk and a plain wooden chair. He sat down and put his pencil and the Ufimtsev paper on the desk before him. There was something else. He'd put it out of his mind, but now it dawned on him—they'd stumble over it as the previous investigator had. But the previous investigator had not been his enemy. The current two men seen by the librarian might well be in league with these auditors.

Everything rested on his proving the diffraction concept!

He almost couldn't concentrate for the burning in his stomach. His head was awhirl. He hardly noticed as a workman came in and began installing a plain black telephone on the desk.

Okay, first things first.

He went out to the parking lot to get his car. Deep in thought, he fumbled for the keys for a minute or two. Then he got in and started to put the key in the ignition.

And froze.

Backing out of his former nose-in parking space was a green Jaguar convertible. The top was down, and looking over his shoulder backing out was a smug Alex Fitch. Sitting beside him was Marsha Kassner. She sat a bit stiffly, with her hands evidently folded in her lap, and her expression was unreadable—she looked comfortable, Paul thought, maybe even amused at something Fitch was saying.

Fitch changed gears and the car rolled forward.

Then Fitch said something clever and Marsha burst out laughing, so much that she held her hand over her mouth for a second. Then she had to reach up and catch her sunglasses before they fell off. They drove away, both talking and laughing at once as if they'd been friends for years.

Paul felt the blow hit him, like a second punch.

Okay, this was not his day. Not his week. Not his season. Not his life.

He sighed deeply as he started the Mustang. Don't die on me, he thought at the car, and it purred smoothly. Of course you won't because I can fix whatever is wrong with you. I can open the hood and fiddle until you're better. I can't do that with Marsha or with these people at work here. But there will be good times again. Somehow. Someday. Somewhere.

At home, Paul made a pot of coffee. He opened a pack of cookies. And he piled his purchases of the previous Friday on the living room table.

As he sipped the hot coffee, and munched on the sweetness of the cookies, he doodled his design for the prototype on a pad. He'd have to build the engine frame himself before he could approach Steve to get any shop work done, like on the inner surfaces.

The windows were open, and the air smelled sweet. It was nice to be home—if he didn't feel so twisted up inside!

There was a knock on the door, and he got up to answer. For a second, he hoped it would be Marsha. But—he glanced at his watch—she'd be back from her lunch date with Fitch—and—well, he had an ominous feeling about her now.

Mrs. Garcia stood before the door, wearing her long gray wool coat and holding her worn black purse. She was a white-haired, heavy-set woman of 60, with a coppery complexion that bespoke her Mexican-American heritage. "Hello, Paul."

"Mrs. Garcia! I thought you gave up on me."

"Do you still need laundry done, and such?"

"More than ever. Come on in." He let her in and closed the door.

"I'm sorry, Paul. I had things to do in the city. My oldest daughter was sick, and I cared for her children. I asked Alberto to tell you, but I guess he must have forgotten."

"That's okay. I have more laundry and dishes than I know what to do with."

"Okay," she said, taking her coat off. "I'll start with the laundry."

The phone rang, and Paul sprang to answer.

"Paul?" It was his dad a retired teacher. Paul's parents now lived in Cocoa Beach, Florida.

"Dad! How are you. How long since we talked?"

As was his custom, Mark was gruff and to the point. "We're fine. I'm a little concerned, son. Some FBI people came around yesterday. It's a good thing your mother was out having her hair done."

"Yeah, they were snooping around the library here too. For all I now, they may be listening in on us." *Geez, am I getting paranoid or what?* "What did they want, Dad?"

"Well, they asked about this and that, you know, and then they narrowed in on your college days. I tried to tell them, 'the boy got straight A's and was on the dean's list every semester.' "

Here it comes.

"Then they zeroed in on that unfortunate situation. I had a feeling those bastards were after that from the start. I tried to tell them it was all a mistake, but they just wanted the facts. Just the facts, sir. Makes me sick."

"Yeah..." Paul nodded to himself. It was coming down the pike, like an express train, and he was going to be run over.

A steady man... Marsha had said. Not a guy who's been arrested, who is about to lose his job, and maybe already has lost his mind to be playing with models.

He tried to reassure his father: "It's probably nothing, Dad. Everything is fine at work. I can't say any more than that about what I'm doing. It's probably just a routine background investigation." He made up a new word: "It's probably a recertification. Yeah. A re-cert."

"Well, I hope so, son. How's the social life?"

Ouch. "Well, I went down to San Diego this weekend with a neighbor and her son. Had a great time.

His father's tone got gruffer, like gravel. "Stay away from those divorced women, especially if they have kids."

"This one's a widow, Dad." Why was he becoming defensive about her?

"Well—." For a moment the old man didn't know what to say. "Okay then. You take care, son."

"Okay, Dad. Thanks. Bye."

Why did I not say something like, Love you, Dad? He banished the fleeting thought.

Back to his model. He had three propeller screws. He'd thought about using four, but it would be difficult enough getting three screws to work in perfect alignment. He'd need a little stiffer frame, and that would add weight. Damn! But then again, the chassis might be inert, but it did the fundamental work of holding the entire machine together.

He leapt up. "Mrs. Garcia!"

The elderly woman looked up from a couch littered with clothing. "Yes?"

"Is your husband still doing metals work?"

"Yes."

"Do you think he'd help me out? I need a few little things done— I'll pay him."

She waved. "Sure. Just give him a call."

An hour later, Paul stood in the cavernous interior of A. Garcia & Son, Metals.

Alberto Garcia was a big, solid man, over six feet tall, with wide shoulders and, in his upper years, an equally wide stomach that his pillow-striped gray-black overalls did little to hide. The shop smelled of tar and oil and burning rubber. In one corner, Garcia's son Juan pounded noisily with a hammer on a bar of metal on an anvil while a cousin stood by with welder's mask and torch to put together a wrought iron fence. In another corner, two Garcia cousins were rebuilding an old racing car.

"What can I do you for, Denny?"

Paul held up his drawings. "I need an eighth inch thick sheet of radio frame stamped out with these tokens." He'd marked the shapes he needed cut.

Garcia took the paper in a gloved hand and held it up. He squinted, head back, and flicked the paper several times fighting the wind which wanted to fold it over his fist. "Yeah, we can do this while you wait," he said. "Cost you twenty bucks for the setup and op time. I'll give you the metal free."

"That's nice of you, Mr. Garcia."

While he waited, Paul strolled around the garage. He was watching a young man in oily blue apron turning a series of three foot pipes to create thread on one end, when he had an idea. "Do you have any really fine iron shavings?"

The young man stopped his machine and lifted his safety glasses up onto his head. "Excuse me?"

"Iron filings. Very fine."

The young man grunted something and indicated Paul should follow him. He took off his gloves. The fellow had a shambling, awkward walk, very slow, while he wiped his blackened hands on his apron. He took Paul to a recycling area that had several small, heavily reinforced dumpsters, the kind a truck could lift once a week. There were also several buckets standing around, filled with a mishmash of metal debris—fine shavings, rough shavings, rings of copper and rings of iron.

"Do you have a fine sieve?" Paul asked.

"Sieve?" The young man shook his head as if he'd been hit, but he dutifully strolled to another part of the yard outside, where Mr. Garcia had a stack of large grates to lay over a concrete mixer. "Too big?"

"Yes. Thanks."

Frustrated, Paul returned alone to the buckets. They were heavy. He squatted down and nudged them playfully, trying to think of a solution. He wanted very fine pellets. Maybe this was the wrong place to look. Maybe a place that made electronic components—Yes!

"Here's your work," Mr. Garcia said, handing over a piece of heavy paper folded several times. Inside were Paul's precious model parts. He paid Garcia and walked out, wondering if he didn't belong in the model airplane business instead of nose cones.

The iron would have to wait for later.

When Paul returned home, Mrs. Garcia had left. The house looked sparkling clean. The kitchen counter had not shone like that in months. And he'd forgotten to leave her a check! He slapped himself on the forehead and ran out the door. It was a ten minute drive to her house. He left a check in an envelope for her with a small child who answered the door.

When he got back, Marsha was just pulling into the driveway with Pete. She smiled and waved.

Paul waved, but he had to force a smile.

"How are you, Paul?" she asked as she got out of the car.

Pete got out and ran over. "Hi, Mr. Owens."

Paul picked Pete up and spun him around.

"Come on honey," she called to her son. She looked apologetically at Paul. "He has to eat and then start right up on his homework."

"Cool," Paul said, kind of relieved. "Go on, Pete. Run to your mom."

Apparently sensing something, Pete did as he was told, but with an odd, questioning glance over his shoulder.

Paul went into his house, the paper folder with his new acquisitions under his arm, and opened the door into the garage. Flicking a light on, he treaded his way among sporting toys—bicycles, surfboard, beach ball, skate board, and more—to his work bench. He flicked on the fluorescent lights and put the metal cutouts on the worn wooden surface. Been a long time since he'd worked on a model here. He'd repaired Pete's finger damage on the kitchen table. This was for hard-core model construction. He flicked on the radio, found a station with good rock tunes, and pulled up a stool.

He pulled out his sketch pad and compared the pieces to drawings he'd done earlier. Perfect. Garcia did precision work. *I'm aiming for 25% less return,* Paul told himself. *That's enough to get their attention with the primitive tools I have here.*

He put on safety glasses and inspected his welding kit. Good; he had a full bottle of gas. The first three pieces of the frame had to be perfectly aligned for the rest to fit together properly. He began the assembly by making the most careful measurements. Old Russian saying: cut once, measure seven times. Or was that nine times? How about twelve? When he was absolutely certain that the first two pieces were aligned, he turned on the welding torch and uncurled a short length of flux. He put a few drops of resin on the surfaces and then went to work with flux and torch.

He'd used small wooden dowels of identical length, since he lacked premier shop tools, to prop the stove-ring chassis pieces exactly one inch apart. Now he welded four triangular fins between each level to replace the temporary wooden dowels. At each step, he used small leveling gauges to make sure the alignment was near perfect. Satisfied, he regarded the first result of his work while chewing on a toothpick.

So far so good. What he had now were three plates, each an eighth of an inch thick, held in parallel, so they formed a structure just over two inches high, roughly square at about six inches to a side. In these plates were three matching round holes—that was where the engines would go: three model airplane engines fueled by individual tanks containing a mix of oil and gasoline. It would be noisy, unfortunately— battery powered would be silent, but the batteries needed would be far too heavy. He didn't want a tethered device because even the finest wire would show up in the radar return.

God, he thought, please let this work or I'll be out of a job and likely ruined.

It was slow, painstaking work, and he went about it methodically, often undoing a piece of work rather than continue on. Sometimes he'd do a step three or four times before nodding in satisfaction.

The doorbell rang.

Paul looked at the shop clock. 5:30 p.m.—what to bet it would be old Pete, with the usual question? Paul took off his safety glasses and rubbed his eyes.

The doorbell rang again.

"I'll be right there!"

Time to switch to the FORTRAN code, he thought. If he could get at least one module written tonight, he could bring it to Steve tomorrow and start getting some numbers back for the surface configuration of the prototypes that would have to be built.

"Hi, Mr. Owens!" Pete said, nose to the back screen door.

Paul opened the door, and Pete marched in. "What's up, Pete?"

"I came to see if you want to fly Condor."

"Did you do your homework?"

"Yes, it's all done."

"No math problems?"

"Well—Mom helped me with those."

"Oh, okay. Good. Sure, let's go fly the plane for a little while."

As he sat on the porch, watching the boy run around as the white plane leaped and soared, he felt a kind of sick pleasure. He wanted to see her, even though he knew as sure as that tree over there was attached to the earth that Alex Fitch would be making his move any time now. Funny, how she'd let him tutor Pete, when she was undoubtedly just as good at arithmetic as Paul, being an accountant. Now she was abandoning that strategy—why? No longer interested? Paul hated being paranoid, but right now it was the only kick he had.

Sure enough, Marsha came out after a while. "Hi, Paul!" she said brightly. "Peter, time to come wash up for supper!" She pattered past, wearing her flowery kitchen apron and fluffy slippers. No effort to apply makeup like that other time; that first blush of wanting to impress him was over, huh? But she still did look very fine, Paul thought.

"Nice shoes."

She looked down and laughed. "Trying to cook and clean and raise a kid." She took Pete by the arm. Pete said: "Hey, no strong arm stuff."

Paul laughed.

Pete flew the plane toward Paul, landed it expertly at this feet, and cut the engine. As he brought the controls over, Paul applauded.

"I was looking for you today at work," she said. "I'm working in your building now."

"Yeah... well, I've temporarily moved to another building...to do some consulting for another project."

"Oh." She appeared innocently surprised. "Too bad. I was hoping to say hello. Man, everything is way top secret in that place." She put her hand behind Pete's head to tow him along. "Come on, squirt. See you, Paul."

"See you." Paul watched her as she walked away. Okay. Just friends. Fine. He could still see the snapshot in his mind of the way she and Fitch had driven away laughing together.

Back to work! He ordered himself mentally, snapping out of his disappointment.

Chapter 13.

Over the next few weeks, Paul was deeply immersed in the FORTRAN programs that he needed Steve Rossi to run on the big IBM mainframe.

He spent some hours each day working in the cold, empty office they'd given him. The laughter of secretaries and bookkeepers traveled along the echoing corridors, and he smelled the scent of their perfume, and their cigarette smoke, and he heard the constant clatter of their typewriters, but he lived in a world apart from them.

Steve would pop in every day: "How's it going? Keeping up the old spirit?"

"Sure."

"Got more code that we can get keypunched?"

"Yeah, here." Paul would hand over another sheaf of yellow legal pad papers with fine pencil markings on them. He wrote several thousand lines of code this way. Bit by bit, the stealth system was taking shape—not in steels and plastics yet, but in his mind, in the conceptual constructs formed in the wonder of data processing.

Ben Rich sometimes stopped by too. "We're looking hard at this thing you're doing, Paul. It sounds like it has a lot of promise."

"I'm building a small scale model to give you a taste," Paul said.

"You remember the D-21?"

"Yes?"

"Paul, I just want you to know that I think there is a lot of work coming down the pike for us. The Air Force has a real problem with radar penetrability, and they are farming out some work. I can't say anymore because of your security clearance status, but I want you to know I can't wait for you to come back to work in the plant."

"Thanks. I appreciate that."

In the evenings, Paul would tinker with his model. He had a real personal urgency to get it in front of his management—the results of the FBI investigation were due any day.

Sometimes Pete came over and they'd fly the Condor around.

"I'll build you a plane of your own one of these days," Paul promised.

"Would you?" Pete shouted. "Would you?"

Marsha would appear to take him home, but there was definitely some barrier there now. The thank you's and hello's were distant. Pete came over less and less.

Then, too, one Saturday evening the green Jaguar appeared in the driveway.

Paul heard the honk of the horn and looked up. There, in the last blush of daylight, sat Alex Fitch. Paul heard the familiar slam of her front door, the shout of a final instruction to the baby-sitter in her excited voice, and then the run down to the car with her sweater fluttering over her bare shoulders. She wore a mighty nice black dress that came down to her ankles in folds, and black pumps, and carried a matching purse. First time, Fitch did not get a hug.

A week later, Fitch did. Paul looked away, sick inside.

The next week, Paul didn't look up when the horn sounded.

The program was ready, and Steve and Ben began to analyze the output. Running the program hundreds or thousands of times, each time tweaking the variables a bit, they began to sketch the ideal configuration of a stealth plane. Since the project was not classified, they could bring Paul sketches.

Paul looked at the monstrosity shaping up on paper. It looked like an insect. It looked baleful.

"This will be a nightmare to sell to the Air Force. We don't even know if it's really aerodynamic," Steve said. "This is going to be tough, Paul."

Ben added: "Let's see what the stealth profile is. We can decide our path from there. We'll know if it's worth arguing a case for it."

Paul learned a little more about Alex Fitch from Steve. Paul had not said a word, but Steve seemed to have a sixth sense. "Our pal Alex Fitch, who goes around telling everyone he was an Army officer... well, he was, kind of. His wealthy folks pulled strings. He's the kind of guy that has everything, but if you have something, he's gotta take it from you anyway."

Paul asked cryptically: "What do those kind of people do once they have it? Do they keep it, or throw it away?"

Steve made questioning eyebrows. "What?"

"Nothing. Just thinking out loud."

"I guess if you have a lot of money, you go through a lot of toys."
He shrugged and walked out the door, looking uncomfortable in the
dark suits the auditors were making all of management wear these days.

"That suit isn't you," Paul called out after him.

"Tell me about it," Steve said walking jauntily away.

Chapter 14.

One evening, as Paul came home late, he walked up to his house and found the door slightly ajar.

Funny—he was good at locking up.

Walking warily into the house, flicking on lights, he found things strewn about. Drawers half open. Doors ajar.

Mouth agape, he walked from room to room. Someone or someones had been in here searching for—what?

Hearing a noise in the back, he ran through the house. The kitchen door was open. Paul pushed through the screen door, just in time to see a man's figure running from the radar-like array toward the side of the house.

"Hey!" Paul chased after him.

Around the side of the house, to the front, Paul ran after him.

Across the street in the shadows, a pair of automobile headlights winked on.

Paul ran across the street, closing on the stranger. He still had no idea who the man was, what he looked like.

A car door slammed, and a huge car that might have been a black government vehicle pulled out on squealing tires and drove away. Paul stopped running and waited until his breath came back. He hadn't even glimpsed the license plate.

He limped back to the house, locked the doors, and began an inventory.

Nothing stolen, as far as he could see.

Angrily, he began the long task of folding things and putting them away.

Chapter 15.

Pete came over one evening looking sad. "Hey, Paul." They were on a first name basis now.

" 'Sup, Pete?"

Paul was working on the guts of his model at the kitchen table. Pete sat glumly with his fists against his cheeks over a mug of milk. "Eh!"

Paul said: "What's 'eh!' ?"

"Just 'eh!'"

"I understand. Something are just 'eh!' ."

"It's this Mr. Fitch."

Paul's stomach leaped.

"He doesn't like kids."

"Why?"

"How do I know?"

"But you know?"

"I can sense it. He just kind of pats me on the head and then makes me go away. He doesn't sit down and talk with me the way you do. Or my dad used to." Abruptly, Pete burst into tears. He put his palms over his face and lowered his head to the kitchen table. He cried heartbrokenly in a solid stream for about five minutes, and tears poured over the rims of his hands.

Paul went into the kitchen, got a towel, wetted it with lukewarm water, wrung it out, and returned to squat beside Pete.

When the boy lifted his head, red-faced and sniffling, Paul mopped his face gently. "I know you're hurting inside."

"I wish more than anything in the world that my dad would come back. I know my mom is hurting too. Everything would be so much better."

"Yes. I'm sure it would."

"Mr. Owens."

"Yes?"

"Have you ever kissed a woman?"

"What?"

Pete made emphatic chopping motions with his hands. "I mean, have you ever really kissed a woman? You know, locked lips with her and kissed?"

"Well, I suppose I have, Pete."

"Then why didn't you kiss her when you had the chance?"

"What do you mean?"

"Up there on Palomar Mountain. When you were sitting on that big rock."

"You mean when you came out of the woods, and saw us, and turned around and ran back into the woods?"

"Yeah, that time."

"We might have kissed, but we were afraid you'd be upset."

"Upset!" He made disbelief eyes and mouth. "Upset! I was hoping you'd kiss her. I ran away hoping you wouldn't be too embarrassed." Pete put his hands over his eyes. "That stuff is so gross, like eating Brussels sprouts. But adults do it. I don't understand it." He lowered his hands to his lap and looked at Paul beseechingly. "She is so unhappy, Paul. Sometimes she cries at night. I hear her when I can't sleep. She often told me she was so happy when she and my dad would kiss. So I thought if you kissed her it would make her happy."

Paul cleared his throat. "Well, to tell the truth, I did kiss her. When we got home, and put you in your bed, she walked me over to my house and we looked at the stars a little..."

"...and that made you kiss?"

"Well, it's part of this thing called being romantic."

"You like her, don't you?"

"Yes."

"Then why don't you steal her back from this Fitch guy?" Pete bolted for the kitchen door.

Paul turned in his chair, too dumbfounded to say anything.

Pete had one foot out the door in case he needed to run to safety. "And Fitch hates you!" he whispered in a loud voice. "Fitch says you're a failure."

"Do you think she believes him?"

Pete stopped to bite a finger and think. "He's got her so she doesn't know which end is up. But in her heart I think she likes you better. I know I do." He ran outside. Paul could hear his feet on the wood porch, then on the grass, then nothing. A door slammed. That familiar sound. Then Paul heard the baby-sitter yelling. And Pete yelling back. The silence. Worried, he rose and went to the window and looked out. There, across the fence, a million miles away under the full moon, in Marsha's house, sat a strange elderly woman knitting. And Pete's light went on in his room and that door slammed.

Chapter 16.

In the morning, as Paul sat working some diffraction equations, because he was waiting for the night's computer run results, a man in a dark suit and hat stepped into the door. "Mr. Owens?"

"Yes?"

The man took his hat off and stepped into the room. He closed the door behind him and walked toward Paul, who sat at the only desk, and the only chair. He pulled out a billfold, in which was a badge. "I'm Special Agent John Mandigar of the local FBI office."

They shook hands. Paul's gut gave an ominous twinge.

Mandigar was a person of contrasts. His pale skin contrasted with this overly dark hair as if one or the other were artificial. His eyes were very dark, the pupils gleaming oddly in the cold gray light in the room. His hair was clipped short, in straight lines, even around the ears, which put them in a sort of box—almost a futuristic design.

Mandigar pulled out a notebook which he opened on the desk. He unscrewed a fountain pen and leaned over the desk ready to write. "Mr. Owens, I am wrapping up the field investigation on your TS review. Do you have any questions at this moment that you would like to ask me?"

"How's it going?"

"We'll have a final decision in a week."

"This was all sort of sudden and unusual, wasn't it?"

"Unusual?" Mandigar had thin lips, and they easily contracted into straight lines. His little black eyes blazed. "Mr. Owens, the Government can review anyone's clearance any time."

"Mr. Mandigar, investigations cost a lot of money, don't they? So wouldn't there have to be a reason?"

Mandigar shrugged, sputtering a bit. "Well, yes, though not necessarily."

"A team of auditors came in and found that my hair was too long and I was playing loud music. Disco music. Apparently these guys still live in the Vietnam of the 1960's and they want to get rid of me, so they've triggered this whole unnecessary investigation."

"Well, I wouldn't say unnecessary. There have been a few employees fired for smoking marijuana. Your name was suggested by—some parties—as a candidate to check into. You're clean."

"Who were the parties who searched my house a last week?"

"Mr. Owens, we don't search houses. That requires a warrant, and I see no indication in your file that a warrant was ever requested or issued."

"How can I believe you?"

"I wouldn't lie to you."

"Somebody searched my house."

"Why didn't you call the police?"

Paul stopped and thought. Why hadn't he? "In my situation, Mr. Mandigar, you begin to feel as though the whole world is against you."

Mandigar shook his head lightly. "I don't know what to tell you." He lightly punched his fist on the desk. "There is, however, this major problem. You see, there is a record at your college campus of you being arrested during an antiwar demonstration. You were formally charged, but you were not convicted."

Paul said: "It was absolutely ludicrous. I was on my way to a chemistry class, and I stopped to watch this big brawl between the campus cops and some demonstrators. I was arrested, along with several other students. It took three days to get the witnesses to come forth and say that we had just arrived there, and that we had not been part of it."

Mandigar put his hands in his pockets and swaggered around the room. "Good, Mr. Owens, real good. Why did the original investigation not make a note of it? Because you lied about it?"

"No. I told about it—it's on my application for this job, where they ask if you were ever arrested for any reason. Mr. Niederhauser—that was your predecessor—believed me, and a statement was put into my file, saying that the arrest had been a mistake. Campus police records confirmed it."

"Okay, I'll buy that. The problem is, though, that your presence at that demonstration may in fact mean that you were at other demonstrations. That you were in fact a student demonstrator. That you may have been in violation of various local ordinances and so forth, never mind that you may have been a traitor to your country!"

"I have never had a treasonous thought in my head, Mr. Mandigar.

I don't drink to excess, I don't smoke, I don't use drugs, and I try not to exceed the speed limit."

"Yeah?"

"I just wish all of you would go away and let me do my work. That would be good for my country."

"Okay, Mr. Owens. Lockheed will hear from us in a week or so, and they'll notify you whether you're fired or not."

Mandigar picked up his hat and left the room.

Paul sat in utter silence, except for the faint creaking of the door as a cold wind blew down the corridor.

Chapter 17.

Discouraged, Paul called up Steve Rossi, who came over with Ben Rich. "Come on into my office," Paul said, "and close the door."

They laughed humorlessly looking around at the cold surroundings.

"Sorry I can't offer you brandy or cigars. You can take turns sitting on my chair though."

"This is your place of exile, I take it," Ben said. "One day, it will be as famous as Elba when you return to fight again."

"Yeah, at Waterloo," Paul said. "I need some help."

"What do you need?" they said in one voice.

"I need to tell you what's going to happen with the investigation. I need you to put in a good word for me." He explained about the meeting he'd just had with John Mandigar of the FBI. Both Rich and Rossi reacted with incredulity. Rossi said: "I've known you for several years. I know pretty much where you're coming from. You're one of the best people we have, Paul. We'll go to bat for you."

Ben added: "You understand what's going on here. They're leaning on us, letting us know we need to be on our toes. It's uncomfortable for a lot of people, but this is just a damned nightmare for you and for our team."

"There is something else I need help with." Paul reached into his large desk drawer and pulled out an object he'd made of papier-mâché on a wire frame made of chicken wire stiffened with coat hanger wire.

"What in the hell is that?" Steve Rossi exclaimed, lighting up a cigarette.

"This is the stealth mockup." He held it up, a model about a foot long, which looked like a praying mantis about to leap at its victim.

Ben smiled. "You gonna run around waving that in the air?

Because I don't see how that thing will fly."

"I need you to coat it with the best absorptive material you have. Then I want it back because I have built a machine that will fly it through the air for you."

Ben looked pained. "I can't do that, Paul. You can't take secret materials off the premises."

"I was afraid you'd say that. I was hoping to have some fun flying it around for you."

Ben allowed: "You can bring it in, and we'll have the shop coat it, and then we'll fly it, but we can't tell you the results. We could wink at you, maybe, if all went well."

"Yeah..." Paul nodded dejectedly. "That's what we'll have to do, then."

That evening, he decided to do a little pre-test. He had managed to obtain a small amount of ferrous oxide in a paint base from an electronics supply house. Iron was a radar-diffractive metal; so was aluminum.

Before doing anything, he used one of his ancient surplus state police hand-held traffic radar guns to shoot the bird, and it showed up very large on his green cathode ray tube display.

He would shoot the bird from the side—the whole plane had a complex shape, but the sides were the least difficult. It did not have to be perfect. All he had to demonstrate was some effect.

First, he glued fine strips of aluminum foil to the surfaces of his model. It took several hours just to get a flat, perfect fit. There must be no perpendicular lines that could show up, so he folded the aluminum over the model's port side.

He had built the model up with material cut from egg cartons. As was standard with stealth construction, he'd put zigzagging 45 degree spars inside, made of aluminum foil covered balsa wood, and filled with sawdust—all strategies to absorb some of the radiant energy that would penetrate there after the coatings broke it up.

Last, he applied a paint of ferrous oxide to coat the central portion of the fuselage.

Even before the paint dried, he was ready.

He took a deep breath, said a prayer, and pulled the trigger on his radar gun.

Alarmed, he looked at the cathode ray display and saw there was no difference.

It didn't work.

Dejectedly, he shifted his stance, ready to drop the gun and give up, when he heard a rustling sound.

The display had changed. The rustling was the sound of the temperature inside the tube changing as a different display painted inside.

There was a shimmering, fuzzy halo around a dark patch.

Paul whooped.

Stealth worked!

He propped the gun up with a stack of books and went to get a beer.

Wonderful, he thought. Wonderful!

The radar return on the model looked as though someone had shot a hole through the plane. It was stunning—though he figured it was only a 20% effect at best. With a professionally done model, it would be much better.

Much, much better. He grinned and toasted the model.

Next morning, he brought the model to work. He met Ben and Steve in his office again. Steve, interestingly enough, wore not the dark suits of recent, but a brand-new three-piece baby-blue polyester suit.

Paul locked the door and put the model on his desk. "I'm going to ask you to give me the drive portion back when you're done. I want to give it to a little boy who lives in my neighborhood."

"Sure, Paul. Should we be laying odds here?"

"It worked last night. I tested it at home."

"That's—incredible, Paul," Ben said.

"I made it from scratch—I got a 20% reduction on a test spot."

Steve whistled. "That's impressive!"

"I want to show you how this works. It's going to be a bit noisy in here." He grinned. He'd built a somewhat crude control box of unpainted plywood. He'd already ensured that all three engines full fuel tanks. "Ready?" He pressed the three magneto connections one by one, and one after another the three powerful mid-size model airplane engines whipped into life, turning three propellers, each with a six inch wingspan.

All three engines pointed straight up. Each had a power damper that could increase or decrease the power through a ten percent range.

That was enough to control the plane.

Ben and Steve smiled like little boys when the model rose slowly off the table and hovered about three feet above the desk. Papers flew everywhere.

Someone pounded on the door.

Ben opened it slightly, listened to a question, and nodded. He yelled above the deafening whine of the model: "Everything is fine here. We are drilling a hole through the wall and should be done in about fifteen minutes."

Steve walked around the model with sparkling eyes and arms open in worship. "Paul, I've always known you were great, but this is the most beautiful thing I've ever seen."

Ben said dryly: "Yeah, and it appears to have some aerodynamic properties."

Paul held the box in both hands and nodded excitedly. "Look. Picture the three engines. They form a triangle pointing forward. Right now, she's stable at three quarter power. If I goose the two rear engines equally—and I built a special switch for that—she goes forward."

The model moved forward, accelerating like a cake of soap squeezed by someone in the shower.

"Ooops!" Quickly, Paul reduced the rear power and upped the front. The model slowed and came to a hovering stop inches by a wall.

"Don't crash it or the shape will be distorted."

Paul flew it back to the desk and landed it. He cut the engines.

In the grayish blue light, oily smoke roiled around the three men's heads. The silence almost hurt more than the noise a moment ago.

Paul said: "You'll have to buff off the coatings I put on last night and then put on your best stuff. It's loaded inside with sawdust, aluminum, all the good stuff. Go test it, guys, and don't let anyone see that shape!"

Ben said: "Paul, if the radar return works as well as that model flies, and if we get the kind of results you say you got at home last night, you're going to be a hero around here."

Paul said: "I'm going to go home and go for a bicycle ride."

Steve set the model back in its bag. "We'll try to move quickly."

Ben said: "We should have some results by tonight."

"Tonight?" Paul asked. "You're going to stay and work on it?"

Steve grinned and shook Paul's hand. "Full bore, my friend. We're both excited as hell. Oh, by the way. Things may be looking up for you."

Chapter 18.

That afternoon, Paul went for a long bike ride—nothing like his marathon several weeks ago, but a good workout.

He returned home, took a shower, and sat on the back porch. His face throbbed with wind burn, and his muscles protested, especially his calves. But he was feeling better than he had in the two months of this nightmare.

There was a point you reached...

He heard someone running and turned his head just in time to see an elated Pete running by with his hand in the air. "Paul! Slap me five, man!"

Paul held out his hand, and he and Pete did a little modified dap— palm on palm, back of hand on back of hand, fingers interlocking, fingers this way, that way...

"What are you so happy about, Pete? Get an A on your arithmetic quiz?"

"Better than that," Pete said, tongue on one side of his mouth, as he slapped Paul's hand around a little more.

"You kissed a girl."

"Stop that. Fitch is history."

"What?"

"Yeah. They had a big scene and he walked out."

"You don't say."

"I do say." Too excited to think about Condor, Pete ran back home, holding his arms out at arms' length and making loud airplane engines. Several times he made chattering machine guns as he strafed the enemy Fitchoids on his way back into the house. The door slammed and all was silent.

Paul rose, dusted himself off, and went inside.

Evidently, when the rich boys played, they left the pieces behind. Paul wasn't interested in picking those pieces up.

The call came at eleven that night. Paul was in bed, reading, when the phone rang. He picked up. "Hello?"

It was Ben Rich. "Paul, it's spectacular. I want you in here first thing in the morning. Kelly Johnson isn't completely sold yet, but we're both going in the morning to shake up some four star generals about ending this nightmare. We need you on the job tomorrow."

"Wonderful."

"Oh, and Paul? This project is about to become extremely classified. Don't talk to anyone, you hear?"

Chapter 19.

In the morning, as Paul pulled out of his driveway, Marsha was walking to her car with Pete. Out of reflex, Paul gave a little wave. Marsha had a funny, dark look—she seemed not to see him. Pete stared after Paul.

Paul drove to the plant, parked far from his old spot, and walked to his barren office. The walk would do him good, he thought defiantly. He'd park far away every day to get the exercise.

Steve popped in a while later. "Kelly and Ben are seeing some of the top Air Force brass. We should have you off the hook in a few days."

"That's great."

"We're going to have a hell of a challenge selling your concept, Paul. Even Kelly is still a little skeptical, but I think in his heart he's on board with us."

"Thanks."

"Got another tidbit of news for you."

"Yeah?"

"Your old bosom buddy, Alex Fitch. He's quit and gone over to Northrop."

"No. My heart bleeds."

"That's not all of it. One of our ex-employees is suing the Government, Lockheed, and Fitch for a number of things, including battery."

Paul closed his eyes. "Let me guess."

"Some woman. Nice looking babe, actually. Name of—." He snapped his fingers twice, couldn't seem to remember.

"Marsha Kassner."

"Yeah, that's her name. How did you guess?"

"She is my next door neighbor. They've been seeing each other, I guess."

"Yeah. I didn't get the full story, though you know how rumors fly around, like what he may have done to her. Our boy got a better offer at Northrop and they snapped him up. So—."

"What did you mean by 'ex-employee?' "

"I dunno. It's common knowledge that she resisted his advances, and he was her boss, so he wrote her up, papered her file, and prepared the way to fire her. Kinda the same bullshit you've been going through, in a way."

"Excuse me, Steve, I gotta run home. I forgot to bring my lunch."

"We'll take you out to a fine restaurant to celebrate, Paul."

"Not today, Steve. I think something else is what I need."

He drove home, heart pounding in his chest, hoping she was there.

He pulled into her driveway, ran up to the house, and pounded on the door.

After a moment, someone yelled: "Go away!" distantly, in the back somewhere.

"Marsha, it's me, Paul."

"Go away!"

"I just want to talk with you. Please."

After a minute or so, the door knob rattled hesitantly. A dark crack appeared, and a faint face. "Paul?"

He gently pushed, and the door yielded, swinging open. She stood with her head down, her arms hanging.

Paul put his arms around her back and pulled her toward him. She slumped against him limply. For a moment, he thought she'd fainted. But her arms rose and her fists rested loosely on his shoulders. She'd been crying, and now big drops again fell down her cheeks. Her hands were cold and she held a soaked hankie in one. "I deserved what I got."

He helped her to the couch. "No, no, no. Nobody deserves to be hurt like that."

She breathed: "I'm sorry."

She looked haggard, aged.

"I'm going to put on a pot of tea. Funny, I don't even know where you keep things because I've hardly ever been in here."

"You don't want to be here."

"Why? Are you radioactive or something?"

"You deserve better."

He put cups on the table while the kettle began to make popping noises. He had the gas on full blast. "Really? You mean the woman I'm looking at right now wasn't good enough for Jeff Kassner?"

She slammed her fist down ineffectually. "Stop that!"

"No, I think we deserve an answer here."

"Did you come to torment me too?"

"Oh stop being a martyr, damn it." He pulled tea bags out of a yellow pot on a shelf. "I want you to think about what I just said. If I recall correctly, you are the woman Jeff Kassner loved. You are the woman who Pete tells me cries herself to sleep some nights over losing Jeff Kassner."

"Please, Paul, don't..."

Nothing to do now but wait for the water to boil.

He let her cry for a few minutes—weak, broken sobs. She'd been crying a lot, and was tiring out. When the kettle began to scream, he yanked it off burner, poured, turned off the heat, set the kettle down, and picked up the tray he'd prepared. He carried the tray to the table, noting how similar the layout of their homes was. He wondered if the layout of their hearts was as congruent.

She sat on the couch, hiccoughing a little, kneading that soaked hankie in both hands.

He pointed at her: "So are you going to tell me that Jeff Kassner was wrong? Jeff Kassner had bad taste in women? If you're saying that, then I disagree with you. I agree with Jeff Kassner, who had great taste in women."

"Oh Paul, you silly man." She sighed.

"Luckily, I happen to agree with Jeff Kassner. His taste and mine are fairly similar, and I trust my judgment."

She slid close to him, rested one hand on his chest, pressed her head against his side. "Would you hold me for a minute?"

"Sure." He embraced her, worked her so she was before him, rubbed his cheek against her hair, and stroked her back, and the back of her head, with his palms. She still had a little of that coconut-fresh scent. "You smell the way you did when I took you to San Diego."

She sniffed. "That was the most wonderful weekend I've had in years."

"We can do it ag—."

She clamped a hand on his mouth. "Don't. I can't handle anything more than going from one moment to the next."

"Okay," he said, gently brushing her hand aside. "Let's do tea."

They sat in silence. It seemed there was so much to say, but there was a woundedness about the moment that filled the whole house with melancholy. The very air was like thick, noxious quicksilver.

"I was in a car accident once," she said, "and I was still in shock hours later, sitting at my parents' table. That felt kind of like this. Who told you I cry at night?"

"Pete."

"My son Peter was sharing confidences with you?"

"Yup."

"When, may I ask?"

"Oh, couple of weeks ago he came running over. I guess he escaped from the baby sitter. Remember the time we were sitting on that rock on Mount Palomar? I was going to kiss you but then Pete saw us and ran back into the woods? He told me he did it because he was hoping I'd kiss you. Apparently you were telling him how much you enjoyed kissing with Jeffrey—I'm sure it was a lot more than kissing—and he just wanted to see you happy for a change."

She shook her head in wonder.

"I gather he also developed a healthy hatred for Alex Fitch."

"Don't mention that name unless we are in a court of law."

"I'd rather not mention him again, if it's okay with you. He and his buddies nearly ruined my career."

"He told me."

"I know he did."

"How do you know?"

"Pete."

"What don't you know?"

"What I don't want to know, so don't start telling me."

"I'm all cried out so this is probably the best time to say it. He tried to rape me. I was not happy with him from the very beginning, and I was going very slow."

Paul was silent.

"I couldn't see that he was rotten to my son, for which I will long hate myself."

"Don't. Don't be hard on yourself."

"I feel so ashamed that I had such poor judgment."

"You are a bereaved widow. You have the right to make a few mistakes."

"Now what do you mean by that?" she said leaning close with a weary smile.

"Nothing at all. I'm not ready right now and neither are you. But next time I go to San Diego, I want to take you along."

"I'm going to be moving back to Oregon, I'm sorry. I've had it with sunny Southern California."

"Would you do yourself and your son a favor and wait a while? Let your feelings settle down?"

She shook her head. "I don't think so. My mother is very ill, and my place is up there. Peter will grow up where I grew up and my parents grew up. I think that's important."

That night, he watched until Pete's light went out, then a half hour later, her light. He dialed her number.

"Yes?" she said in a tired, husky, unhappy tone.

"I'm lonely over here."

"Oh?" She seemed to brighten a little.

"Yes. I've been through the wringer the past two months, and I think things are starting to get back to some semblance of reality."

"I'm glad to hear that."

"So I just thought I would kiss you. It's been prescribed for both of us."

"Hmm," she murmured, "I think you'd better bring that medication over here."

The prospect of losing each other again soon—for good—made what time they would have all that more intense and precious.

She showed him Pete, who was sleeping on his side with his chin pulled up and his mouth slightly open, illumined by an otherworldly faint bluish light.

She put a finger over her lips and gently tucked her son in.

Then she took Paul's hand and led him down the hall to a larger bedroom. He'd never been in here, and he noted the frilly four-poster bed with a little surprise. She turned off the lights—even the hall light—so that the room was steeped in that same faint blue haze.

As he undressed, he realized suddenly that she had swept off her nightgown, revealing her full, firm breasts. Her skin was smooth to his touch. Her fingers roamed eagerly around his head, in his hair, down his back. His palms roved along her curves, feeling the downy skin, the firmness of her buttocks. He leaned down and kissed one puckered nipple, then the other, and she inhaled sharply each time. Slowly, sweetly, they drifted to the bed, and there they found the wild pleasure each had missed for so long.

Chapter 20.

Paul returned to work and met with Ben Rich, Steve Rossi, and several engineers.

Ben said: "We know there is a crisis on about radar. The Government is all over aerospace, trying to get fixes. We're so secret that we didn't even get the RFP (Request For Proposal), and the RFP is so secret only a few people at a few companies knew about it.

"We haven't built a fighter since Korea, and our main customer has been the CIA. I've had to jump through hoops to get them to let us talk to the Air Force about the work we've done on spy planes like the U-2 and the SR-71 Blackbird—all highly classified and for years we denied they existed.

"We want a piece of that anti-radar money, Paul, and we were thinking about floating a manned version of our D-21."

Paul knew what that was: a series of pilotless ramjet drones, 44 feet wide and manta ray shaped, that the Air Force launched from B-52 bombers at high altitudes to photograph nuclear missile test facilities and ranges. It had a very low radar cross section.

Ben continued: "We've put together a small team to noodle through the possibility of reconfiguring the design, maybe to include a pilot. The problem is, the seed money is already used up—a million bucks to come up with a proof of concept—and Lockheed will have to eat the bill if we go ahead. So I'm deeply interested in your idea. The little model was a real heads-up, and we're going to build our own models in house. If that works, we'll consider putting our money on your project. You'll be right in the thick of it, Paul."

"Thanks!" Paul's heart went wild with elation.

"Your early computer results look intriguing, and we want you to go ahead full time, whatever it takes, to nail down the optimum configuration so we can build a model. Got a surprise for you—we've called back Bill Schroeder as a consultant."

"Wow!" Great—Bill had been Paul's mentor over the past few years. A brilliant mathematician, Bill was in his eighties and retired now, but his mind was as sharp as ever.

"We have a program name for you—Echo I. How long do you think you might need?"

"Four months," Paul replied unhesitatingly.

Ben shook his head. "Can't do it. Three months."

"All right. Three months. After what I've just been through, that sounds like kid stuff."

The men all laughed.

One engineer said: "Paul, I don't know the math on this, but I can tell you that there has never been a plane like the one you're building. I'm really puzzled about how we're going to telescope 5 or 10 years of development to put together this entirely new class of aircraft." He sounded straight, but there was an undertone of disbelief or even ridicule in his tone.

Ben said: "If we go ahead, we'll have to use off the shelf components. You bring up a good point. Why don't you start putting together some theoretical configurations using stuff that's already in use—different engines, instrument panels, wheel assemblies, what have you."

"For a plane whose shape we don't even know?"

"You saw the model. It'll kinda look like that. Come on, you guys, this is the Skunk Works, not some tight-ass conventional shop. Even a brick will fly if you put the right engines and wings on it. Make me a flying brick."

The man grinned. "You got it, boss."

After the meeting, Steve Rossi walked with Paul to Paul's new office—his old laboratory! All of his boxes were lined up along the wall, just as the usurper Alex Fitch's boxes had been only a few months ago. And Paul had his old parking spot back.

Now if only Marsha were working here still. But some things were not to be.

Steve said: "You gotta understand, Paul, this is big-time, and Kelly Johnson doesn't seem to like it. The Government doesn't believe in stealth a whole lot. As a nice bit of frosting for the cake, maybe, but they are pushing ahead like gangbusters, billions of dollars of funding, for a bomber called the B-1. The B-1 will fly in a treetop level, lost in ground clutter, and sneak through the radars. That's what the Pentagon is betting on. Turning them around will be an uphill battle every inch of the way."

"At least I have a job and I have my clearance back."

"You're a humble man who asks little." Steve laughed and clapped Paul on the back.

"I've been to hell and back. You should try it some time. It's an eye opener."

"No thanks."

And to heaven and back, Paul added inwardly.

"Oh Paul!" Ben Rich's voice echoed in the hallway.

Paul turned.

Ben walked toward him carrying the undercarriage of the model, with the skin gone. "Figured you might want this back. Looks like a helluva nice design. Three engines, huh?"

"Thanks." Paul accepted the little bird. "I figured three engines would be optimum for stability."

That afternoon, Marsha came over with Pete. She was radiant, though a little sad underneath. Paul wished she'd let him erase all that tragedy from her lovely eyes.

"Look here, Pete. I made a new model."

"Where's the wings?"

"Well, the wings are—at work. It's a big secret and we can't talk about it. So what I figured is, why don't you and I build a nice airplane."

"A flying saucer!"

"Huh? Well, okay, sure... this thing hovers pretty nicely."

"Wow! Three engines! Will it do gyros?"

"You mean gyrations? If we design it right, sure."

"Can we design it right?"

"I'll do my best. Why don't you fly Condor a little bit while I talk to your mom? I'll sketch a little design—hey, I have an idea, why don't you also do a saucer design. Then we'll put the two together and come up with—."

"Condor III," Pete said proudly.

"You got it."

Paul and Marsha went into the kitchen for tea. They stood close together in the gloom, watching the boy run around outside. The tea kettle made popping sounds.

"You're very good with him, Paul." She squeezed his hand.

"I like him. He's a great kid."

"He's a lot like his dad. Big hearted and brave and steady... Jeffrey had so many great qualities."

Paul saw the light. "You're a real great gal, Marsha. You deserve another Jeffrey, not a silly nose cone engineer."

"That isn't it at all. I wouldn't have you in my bed if I didn't—well, think the world of you, maybe even feel some kind of crush on you." She placed the palms of her hands on his chest and rubbed lightly, absently, up and down. "You're a wonderful man. Believe me, Alex Fitch was an eye opener. I've been spoiled. First Jeffrey, and then you."

"He's pretty smooth with women, I guess," Paul said, wishing Fitch had never appeared in their lives.

"I saw through him pretty quickly. He was my boss, and I was new at the company, and I didn't know how to say no. All I knew how to do was put the brakes on, and—we'll, that's old hat."

"So you're suing him?" That would tie her up here for years, Paul thought.

"No. My lawyer said she's dropping the case. It was attempted rape, and he didn't get very far, because I hit him with my shoe. All he did was slap me across the face, and it didn't leave any marks. There's no real proof other than my word, and court would be ugly." She put her palm on his cheek. "We have about ten days, sweetie. I already have the plane tickets, and the house goes up for sale tomorrow. I'm sorry, darling."

"Do they have nose cone designers up in Oregon?"

She smiled wistfully and shook her head. "No. You stay here, build your career, meet a nice girl, forget me—I'm used material."

"I feel very strongly for you."

"I know you do."

The kettle whistled and they went into the kitchen with the tea tray. Paul realized he was upset when he tried to sip scalding tea and burned his lower lip. She dabbed concernedly with a dishtowel. "Poor baby."

"I want to ask you just once, Marsha, and then I will never say it again. Please stay here and let's see what becomes of us."

She shook her head darkly, and he could see the strength of her determination. "My mother is very sick, and my dad is going to pieces. I have to help. She's got a clear mind, and she's been in remission, and I expect she'll be better in a few months. By then our lives will have moved on to other things."

"Is there a man?"

"No." She gazed at him with utter sincerity, and some hurt. "Paul, if there were a man, I would not be sleeping with you."

"I just wanted to know."

"And I never slept with Fitch. I'm sorry if you were jealous. I'll make it up to you in the next few weeks."

Paul realized he was beaten. "All right."

She touched his cheek again. "I have to think about Pete. He has family up there that miss him. And Jeffrey's parents—they desperately want their grandson to live near them. And you're involved in the project of a lifetime, from what I can tell."

"How do you know?"

"Pete told me." She laughed, having put the shoe on the other foot.

"What does Pete know?"

"He's a pretty bright kid. He looks out the window at your comings and goings. He knows you've been through a crisis, and he knows you've been designing secret models. He had it all figured out."

"I can't talk about it."

"Of course not. Don't be silly, Paul. You can't give up what you're doing, and I can't change what I have to do."

"This must be the accountant in you—are all accountants that rational?"

"I'm just starting to be."

"Want to come over here tonight? See my models?"

"I'd be afraid to. After what you told me about intruders breaking in your house and making a mess. I couldn't bear to think of being here with you, and Peter alone in the house if somebody broke in."

Paul nodded. "If you'd like, I'll come over there."

She threw her arms around his neck and hungrily put her lips to his, thrusting at him with her tongue. He nearly dropped his tea. "I want you very badly," she said.

Later that night, when all was still, the phone in Paul's house gave one ring. It was her signal. As he crossed the cool, damp lawn, he looked up into the starlit sky and tried to make a mental snapshot of this moment. He would never be happier than when he was crossing the yard to climb into bed with her. He must remember every one of these precious few days, because they would be gone all too soon. The house across the yard would never seem the same to him—he knew all this because he was old enough, he'd lost enough in life, he knew the ropes. Better enjoy this while it lasted. He'd make love with her three, four times a night trying to store it up like charging some celestial battery in his soul before staggering home through the dew late at night. He'd get up early and come back each morning to make love with her before Pete was awake... only that never happened, because he was always so tired from making love the night before that he'd sleep to the last minute. Luckily, Marsha wasn't working now, and she had a nice hot breakfast waiting for him and Pete every morning. It was all that was left now: to enjoy her while they had each other.

Chapter 21.

Bill Schroeder showed up for work the next morning, carrying his metal lunch pail and unbreakable steel coffee thermos. A spry and robust man with age-mottled skin and thin whispy white hair, Bill greeted him from the door. "Hey there, young feller!"

"Bill!" Paul ran up and hugged his old mentor. He'd learned a lot from Bill about how to tweak and twist the vagaries of abstract mathematics so it would fit around messy everyday engineering problems.

"Are you gonna share your lab with me?"

"I hope so, if you don't mind."

"H-ell no, I consider it an honor. When do we start?"

"How about right now?"

"Something about radar. I just picked up my TS on the way in," he said, pointing to the purple-edged badge with his photo on it.

Paul explained the whole matter to him, starting with the Ufimtsev paper.

Bill whistled. "Good call on that paper. How did you happen to find it?"

"I was browsing through some abstracts and some words caught my attention—electromagnetic waves, diffraction, that kind of thing. I've already run some rough algorithms on the IBM mainframe, but we need to tweak this thing so we come up with the right shape."

"The exact optimum shape," Bill added with purposeful redundancy.

"Exactly." Paul was pleased. They'd always worked well together, and the old magic was back.

Bill took a few hours to study the mathematical construct, beginning with Maxwell's equations and Ufimtsev's summation of the work done since. "A wonderful paper," Bill commented. "Simply lovely. Very elegant."

Steve Rossi popped in to tell them that they would have uninterrupted computer usage 24 hours a day, seven days a week. "We'll need that," Bill said.

Within a week, Bill told Paul: "We're getting a good handle on this." He chuckled gleefully and rubbed his palms together. "Let's surprise these guys and get the job done way ahead of time."

"I'd like that," Paul said.

"Are you nervous at all?" Bill said a while later, looking up over his glasses with a shrewd look, glasses sliding down his nose.

"Yeah," Paul had to admit. More about his personal life, but also about what would happen if this concept fell through. "I'll feel like a fool."

"Bah." Bill waved a hand. "You're young. That's the time to be a fool. Hell, more than one person walking around the Skunk Works has fallen prey to an ambitious but silly idea. If you get egg on your face, join the club." He twirled his glasses. "I don't think so. This whole situation looks great. Let me tell you something." He spread out some computer printouts and, with his pencil, drew diagrams on them. "With this new technology, I think we're going to find that the amount of return is the same, no matter how big the target."

"You're kidding."

"I think not. The amount of return is like a pinprick. A little round dot --a child's marble. Whether you're imaging a roller skate, a bus, or an aircraft carrier, you always get that same little dot."

"Bill, that's fantastic. Wow! Great!" It made sense, now that Bill had pointed it out. Steve and Ben would flip—once they got over their disbelief!

Paul's evenings were deliciously the same. After work, he'd go to Marsha's house for a warm supper, a luxury he had not had in years. *So this is what married life is like,* he thought. *No wonder people do it so much.*

After supper, he and Pete would go out and fly the planes. Sometimes they'd play Dueling Condors. Then they'd go to Paul's living room and draw their designs. With only a week to go, they both knew they'd better speed the process up.

"We're gonna build this extra sturdy so you won't need to do a lot of repairs," Paul said.

"My grandpa Kassner knows a lot about planes. He can fix it if it breaks. But Paul?"

"Yes?" Paul asked as he began to fit a dowel. Using the steel frame Mr. Garcia had made, Paul built a round edge and fitted inward sloping solid balsa pylons in symmetry. Around the outer edges of the balsa, he glued a fine sheet of roofer's flashing tin to protect the soft wood in case Pete ran the saucer into a tree. The plan was to then make a standard balsa crosswork and cover it with doped tissue hardened like a ceramic eggshell.

"Why don't you come with us?"

What could he say? "I wish I could, but I have important work to do."

"What about when you're done?"

"That's a long way off, Pete. And you need to be with your grandparents."

"I know, but—." He made a face.

"I know. I'm sorry. You can come visit me from time to time. I'll always be here for you."

"Thanks."

Later that night, after Pete was asleep, Paul stole across the lawn, as it rained. He lay with Marsha, skin against skin under her quilt, their body heat mingling. They kissed her long and hungrily while water dripped in the eaves outside. His hands roved over comfortingly familiar contours of her body, a jet flying blind by the feel of its radar. He wanted to memorize every inch of her, every curve, every dip and hollow, as if he were building a monument of memory that must last him all his life.

Chapter 22.

Paul noticed a For Sale sign in front of Marsha's house in the morning. The sign sat desolately in the middle of her front lawn.

That morning, Ben Rich arranged a meeting with the aerodynamics team. With Paul and Bill, that made twelve men jammed into a medium size conference room. Several men stood in the corners, others sat on the floor.

Bill Schroeder drew a diagram on the blackboard with a piece of light green chalk. "Gentlemen, the overall design we're zeroing in on looks kind of like this." He drew three figures—a side view, a front view, and a top view—which he connected, in good draftsmanlike form, with point-for-point lines. This way, each point on one view could be matched with itself in each of the other two views.

"She looks kind of like an arrowhead from the top, see."

Already there were sniggers. Experienced design engineers looked at each other shaking their heads, with mocking smiles.

Bill calmly droned on: "From the front, we have this kind of carapace look. The idea, gentlemen, is never to present a straight line or flat surface that is exactly perpendicular to the radar gain.

"From the side, it's kind of a sleek diamond shape. You'll see that the entire surface will be composed of triangle and diamond shapes."

"What is so damn magical about triangles?" one engineer asked.

"Good point. A triangle is that polygon which contains the least number of sides and coincidentally therefore of points. It contains three points, and any two points contain one side. The problem, gentlemen, is that this is 1975 instead of 2075 and our computers are quite limited. If we could process millions or billions of calculations per second, instead of thousands, then we could incorporate curves. I think the day of the curving wing or even flying wing stealth plane may come in our lifetimes."

"So why are we dropping everything to do this?" asked another engineer. He looked around at his colleagues. "I just want to be sure we aren't losing our minds here."

A majority of the men in the room laughed.

Bill shrugged. "Guys, pry open your heads and listen. I didn't come dragging myself in here in my old age to fool around. We stand the chance to revolutionized warfare forever. Right here. Us. In this room." One could hear a pin drop. "We can achieve reductions in radar image by the thousands, by the tens of thousands."

A gasp went around the table. Disbelief.

"We can make a B-52 look tinier than a door knob."

Laughter swelled around the room. Several men turned away holding their heads. At least one started toward the door, and had to be pulled (laughing) back by his shirt tail.

Ben Rich spoke up. "Guys, here's the deal. I'm not going to commit the company unless I can show you and the management proof of concept with a model. All I ask you to do is have an open mind right now. I believe Paul and Bill are wrapping up Echo I way ahead of schedule and we should be ready to build a model very soon. Then we'll be able to actual testing, and you'll all be invited. For now, remember— keep on doing your work, but in the backs of your minds, be thinking about how to make a brick fly. Well, now we know it's going to be more like an arrowhead."

That evening, Paul and Pete finished the balsa framing on the model and took it outside for doping. That meant stretching sheets of tissue over every opening, and then repeatedly applying coats of a special glue, letting each coat harden before applying the next. Paul was hurrying the project along as much as he could, even after Pete went to bed. He applied the last coat for the night around ten, threw his clothes in the wash, and took a shower.

Marsha wrinkled her nose later that night in the dark as she crept on top of him and smelled his hair. "Have you been with another woman? You smell like fingernail polish."

He tickled her. She twisted behind him, squealing and giggling.

"That's the smell of airplane dope."

"I know, silly. I'm so happy that you're doing this for him."

Chapter 23.

Next morning, Bill told Paul: "I think we're ready to give them a preliminary configuration. We can continue refining and pruning, but I think we're at the 95% range now."

"That's 95% reduction, right?" Paul asked facetiously.

"Young man, what do you think we're doing here, playing horse's asses?"

Steve and Ben were excited when Bill and Paul went to tell them the news. Steve said: "I'll have a team of draftsmen go full time on three views. I'll have a model making team work on the guts of it."

"Yeah," Paul chimed in, "I wanted my model to fly to add some badly needed wow-factor for a little boy and a woman I care about. This time, I want us to mount this baby on a pylon and show the engineers what it can do."

Paul went home at lunchtime to see Marsha. First, he applied several coats of glue to finish the doping. The fuselage was by now hard as plastic. It would take some beating, and he'd teach Marsha how to help Pete patch it if he put any holes in it.

"Thanks for coming by," she murmured as they lay together in bed.

"I want to spend every moment I can with you."

"That's nice." She stroked his hair. "I'm yours for as long as I can stay."

"Maybe..." he started, but she put a finger over his lips.

"Honey, you have your life here with your planes and nose cones.

I have mine in Oregon. I don't want us pining for each other. Sometimes we have to be strong in life and do what's right. Especially when we've done what's wrong."

He looked down at his hand, which rested on her breast, which was soft and warm, like jelly. She wrapped one arm around him from behind and pulled him onto her. "Take me," she said through gritted teeth, "take me now."

Back at work, Paul stopped in at the plant so see what the model makers were up to. A ten foot wooden model was taking shape on a long table in the cavernous hangars where, during World War II, P-38's had rolled off the production line.

By now, insiders were referring to the concept as The Diamond.

Someone—perhaps Ben Rich—was calling it the Hopeless Diamond, in a twist on the name of arguably history's most famous diamond. Hadn't the Hope Diamond, like King Tut's tomb, killed everyone who'd gone near it? Paul wondered if the reversing of the name might imply a different fate for those near the Hopeless Diamond.

"She'll be ready to test tomorrow," one of the technicians told Paul.

Paul went away whooping, but he was full of butterflies.

Tomorrow would tell the tale!

That evening, Pete was suitably awed.

"We are ready to take our first test flight," Paul announced. "One little coat of primer, like so—" (he walked around the flying saucer, which sat on a sawhorse in the back yard) "—and she'll be dry by the time we finish supper."

Holding Marsha around the waist, and Pete by the hand on his other side, he walked to her house.

"I made meat loaf," she said. "You said it's your favorite."

"Yes."

They talked and laughed and ate.

The September sun showed signs of going away a little earlier.

"We'd better get out there," Paul said, wiping his lips.

"Yeahhhhhh!" Pete said, rushing to the door, and his *yeah* trailed out onto the lawn after him.

Marsha stood in Paul's back yard, arms folded, as Paul and Pete fired up the bird.

"Here," Paul said, handing her a tiny bottle of some cheap liqueur he'd picked up on impulse at the drugstore. "You have to christen her."

"Oh okay, what are we calling her?"

"Condor III," Pete yelled.

"Okay," Marsha said, "here goes. I dub thee Condor III." She tapped the bottle against the plane, and of course it didn't break. "What do I do now?"

"I don't know," Paul said. "It's supposed to break on the bow. The rule book isn't clear."

"That's for ships," Pete yelled. "This is a plane. You don't break bottles on planes. You fly the bottle and serve it to the passengers."

"That's it," Marsha said. She placed the bottle on top of the saucer.

Paul noticed a flash of light out of the corner of his eye, but ignored it in the excitement. "Good going." He shook Pete's hand. "Captain, take her aloft."

"Aye aye, matey!"

Pete delicately worked the controls. Condor III, a flying saucer a foot in diameter and about eight inches thick, slightly more rounded on top than on the bottom, lifted smoothly.

"Keep the controls together so they are all on the same power level." He wished now he'd built in more sophisticated controls.

But Condor III wasn't hard to fly at all, as long as one made changes slowly. She swung around a corner, and the little bottle fell off, lost forever in a mass of clover.

"Well," Marsha said, "there goes the passenger. He'll sleep it off."

Pete brought Condor III in to a smooth landing. They refueled the three cells and sent her up. This time Pete took her up to rooftop level.

"Careful," Marsha said.

"As long there isn't a wind gust," Paul said.

But Pete brought her back down without any trouble. "She flies like a dream."

"She's all yours."

"Thanks, Paul."

Marsha kissed Paul.

Across the street, somewhere, a car pulled out and drove off, its headlights stabbing the road ahead of it.

Chapter 24.

About ten a.m. the next morning, September 14, 1975, Ben Rich called a meeting of those who were working, or might be working, on the Hopeless Diamond project. They met in a drafty corner of the old main hangar, where a ten foot mockup of the plane sat on a crude pylon consisting of four 2x4x4's attached to a plywood base.

The plane was starting to look rather beautiful in its hooded, sinister way, Paul thought.

About twenty persons crowded in a semicircle around Ben and the mockup.

100 feet away, Steve Rossi supervised a crew of technicians working on a small radar source.

"Okay," Ben announced. "Your attention. You are about to see my personal proof of concept. Are you ready, Steve?"

Rossi waved—thumbs up.

Kelly Johnson stepped next to Ben and announced dourly: "Ben and I bet each other a quarter about this contraption. He says it will outdo the D-21 drone, which has the lowest radar signature of any plane to date."

The men laughed, some with a tinge of derision.

Ben held up a quarter and walked up and down like a challenger in a boxing match. "In a few minutes, we're going to change the nature of warfare."

The corner grew quiet.

Steve signaled.

"Ready?" At Steve's answer, Ben nodded. He pointed to a cathode ray tube on a stand nearby. "Gentlemen, you see that gadget? Watch the screen." He took a few steps out. "See that van parked about 200 feet away? Let's test our equipment. Shoot the van, please."

The technicians turned their gun and aimed it at an old blue van parked against the wall.

"Look at the return."

On the screen, Paul saw a large bright blotch. As the timer swept around the face of the readout, the bright blotch kept showing up regularly.

"We have a big fat van on our radar screen. Now, gentlemen, we're going to aim at our model here and let's see what happens."

Paul had butterflies. This was it, the deciding moment. Even though Ben said he'd already seen the results and was bullish, Paul was filled with a sense of dread. What if it failed?

The men watching the screen began to grow restive.

One yelled to the shack: "You guys need some help?"

"Your aim is off," another yelled.

"Is it plugged in?" a third quipped. Laughter.

Steve Rossi yelled back: "It's been on for several minutes. Look closely at the tube."

The men crowded in—all laughter now silent—and stared.

"There is nothing!"

"Wait, I see something!"

"That thing's broke!"

"No, there." Ben pointed to a tiny pinprick, a single pixel of light so small it was lost in the brightness of the sweep itself against the darker green background field.

A babble of amazement rose.

"No way!"

"Come on," Ben said, "I'll let you each try it out. That's the only way you're going to believe this." He gave Paul and Bill a thumbs up and a wink. "Great job," he whispered.

There were still guffaws of disbelief.

"Okay," Ben said patiently, "let's make this a real benchmark. We're going to have Steve fetch the wooden mockup of the D-21, and we'll shoot them side by side."

Some of the men straggled away, because they had work commitments. About ten persons, including Paul and Bill, remained for the half hour it took to pull the wooden drone model out of storage and wheel it next to the Hopeless Diamond model on a technician's tool cart.

The D-21's manta-ray shaped body filled the radar screen like an electrified advertisement. The Hopeless Diamond remained nearly invisible.

"The best part," Ben announced, "is that these results exactly fit the calculations made by Paul and Bill."

Applause pattered from the crowd—no more derision.

"But the most amazing part is that the signature—no bigger than an eagle's eye—is the same no matter how big or small the target."

More applause.

Paul felt an intense relief wash over him.

That evening, as Pete rode his bicycle up and down the sidewalk and both driveways, Marsha said: "You have a glow about you." She and Paul sat on his back porch. She had made lemonade.

"I had a great day." Paul checked out Condor III from all sides.

"I know, you can't tell me about it."

"Yup. Tell me about you. How was your day?"

She hesitated. "I had an offer on the house."

"Oh?" He tried not to show his distress.

"I decided to accept, and we're going into escrow. That means I might be free and clear as early as next week."

"I see." He did not want to ask the obvious question, but she answered it for him.

"We're leaving on Monday, Paul." She looked down.

"I'll miss you."

"I'll miss you too."

"I said I wasn't going to say anything more, but you know that I'll keep my door open for you down here if you change your mind."

"Don't, Paul. It's the worst thing you can do. I'm not coming back. Not ever. Don't waste any time. Please. I do care about you, more than...anyway...and I wish you the best."

"Thanks."

He excused himself and went to the bathroom. Through the lace curtain, as he sat, he saw here walk across the lawn to her house, looking anxiously for Pete. "Peter!" she called. "Peter!"

Pete came streaking around the corner on his bicycle, laid it down by their back door, and hugged her. Together, they went inside.

Paul sat in the bathroom and held his head in his hands, feeling as if he'd been hit by a car. If there ever was a time he wanted to cry, it was now. No tears came. Just an awful gray feeling, like a load of wet concrete weighing him down.

Some time later—he had no idea how long—he heard her voice at the kitchen screen: "Paul, honey, want to come over and eat?"

"Yeah."

As he tidied up in the living room, more to regain his composure, he held up Condor III and looked at it from all angles. Good job there, he told himself. Pete would have a good time with it. He'd take it over to their house. Where was the control panel? Oh, over there in the corner. He did a few dishes, washed his face to be fresh, and went out the door.

"Hi," she greeted. She'd set a fine table. "My china is all gone, packed, but I have these plastic plates that are imitation china."

"Smells great," he said, kissing her, to Pete's approving look.

Paul ate quietly. He couldn't talk about his triumph at work today, whose luster had dimmed considerably because of her words, and he didn't want to talk about their trip north. Sensing that, Marsha looked down at her food a lot and ate slowly, sparingly, as if she didn't have much appetite. Paul ate hungrily, but not tasting much.

"Wonderful meal," he said afterwards, and they held hands across the table but didn't look at one another much.

"Paul, where's Condor III?" Pete asked.

"Oh, I was going to bring it. It's on my living room table."

"Can I go get it?"

"Sure. I told you, it's yours."

"Be careful, sweetie," Marsha said.

Chapter 25.

Pete felt a sick feeling in his stomach as he let the screen door bang shut behind him. The night was dark and full of secrets, full of promise. He just didn't get it. If they liked each other so much that they were holding hands and kissing, then why didn't they just stay together? It could be like this forever—two houses side by side, nice evening meals, model airplanes... adults were impossible to figure out.

Crickets chirruped and tiny animals stirred in the bushes.

Across the street, a pair of automobile headlights came on. They were aimed at the front of Paul's house.

Pete held up his hands to shield his right eye from the intensity.

He heard a deep, heavy engine rumble. He heard the crackle of tires on gravel as the car moved.

Pete moved behind the house, where it was thankfully dark.

He rounded the corner and got to the porch.

He stepped up onto the porch and walked up to the door.

He turned the worn round knob and pulled the door open.

He stepped inside and reached for the kitchen light.

He was not alone in the house.

Someone was walking around in the living room—he heard muffled footsteps, ragged breathing—heavy, a man's—and saw the beam of a flashlight stabbing around.

Pete flicked the light switch. A second later he realized he should run.

The flashlight beam in the next room went out.

Pete stepped forward hypnotically, attracted by curiosity.

The kitchen light lit the living room in a half light.

A big man dressed in black, with a ski mask over his head, had Condor III under his arm and was about to turn away.

"Hey!" Pete yelled. "That's mine! Give that back!"
Pete ran and grabbed the model as the man tried to back away.
The man shoved Pete, sending him staggering toward the kitchen.
Then something hit Pete in the back, and everything went black.

Chapter 26.

Paul frowned. "Did you hear something?"

She was just sitting in an attitude of abject reflection, sort of curled in on herself. They were holding hands on the kitchen table, sitting shoulder to shoulder, wrapped in light that reflected in a gentle glare from the oilcloth, and around that the darkness that filled the house.

They heard a loud bang, like a door slamming.

Paul rose. Marsha jumped to her feet. They ran out the door and across the lawn.

As they sprinted across the lawn, they heard a car roar away, spraying gravel against the front of Paul's house.

They bolted around the corner and up onto the porch.

A body lay in the entrance between the kitchen and living room.

Pete.

Marsha screamed.

Paul crashed the door open, slid across the floor, and skidded to a halt next to the boy.

Marsha followed, on her knees, shrieking.

Pete's head lay in a splash of blood.

Paul felt the boy's neck. Where was the pulse?

He leaned over and listened for breathing.

"He's not breathing," Paul said, "Call 911."

Wailing desperately, she didn't hear. She tugged at her son, who was completely limp.

Paul jumped up. He grabbed the phone. His hands shook and his fingers nearly missed as he dialed: 9, 1, 1...

The emergency operator answered, a woman with an even, nasal voice.

Paul said: "I have an eleven year old boy here who's unconscious, bleeding from a head wound, I think caused by burglars, and I don't know if he's alive or dead."

"Your location?"

Sheriff's Deputy Jeff Toole, a big blond man of thirty, was nearing mid-shift and was about to go to dinner when the call came in about a possible violent crime at the home of—wow, Paul Owens! The guy who couldn't remember to bring the library books back. Man, Jeff thought as he turned on the lights and siren and headed for the other end of Madeira. This would be a big deal. Owens was one of the whiz kids from Rockwell that every cop in the area knew about and had to keep an eye on.

Paramedics Clint Young and Shep Frizzell were reading magazines at the ambulance station when the call came in about a possible bleeder, maybe a burglary victim, shooting or other status unknown, at an address on Madeira Road.

Within a minute, the white ambulance pulled out of its garage, lights and sirens wailing.

At Burbank's Fire Station 99, the Emergency Unit rolled out, followed by a small hook and ladder. Red lights flashing, sirens howling, the vehicles roared out of the fire house and into the black of night.

At every intersection, the driver sounded a loud klaxon like a Norse war god's horn.

Everywhere, cars pulled to the side as the two red engines blared through the streets, one closely following the other as they wove through traffic, sometimes cutting through corner gas stations.

Deputy Jeff Toole was the first on the scene.

His squad car plowed to a sideways halt on Owens's front lawn.

Jeff left the door open, scrambling to the trunk, where he pulled out the emergency first aid kit.

Marsha cradled Pete to her as she sat on the floor. Crying brokenly, she rocked back and forth sideways, holding his head over her shoulder as if he were a baby. His arms hung limply at his sides.

Paul pull him away to try mouth to mouth.

As he blew into Pete's mouth, the boy coughed.

Marsha held her hands before her face and looked on in shock. Hope poured over her features, obliterating grief.

The door crashed open and a policeman staggered in, carrying a heavy metal case.

Toole—Paul recognized him—no time to talk now.

Two paramedics hurried in, carrying more emergency equipment. Toole made way for them as they bent over the boy.

Pete coughed again, convulsively.

Several firemen in long black helmets and bulky orange rubber suits entered the house.

"He's breathing," one of the paramedics noted. "Pulse is acardic, slow."

Pete coughed again.

The firemen were soon on their way back to the station.

Paul stood and held Marsha, who pressed her face against his side in the shelter of his arm.

One paramedic worked on Pete while the other went outside and came back pulling a stretcher.

The paramedic carefully felt Pete's body, starting from the head down, and spoke as he did. "He's got a pulse, coming back now. Looks like he was struck on the head. I checked his pupils and they are a little unfocused but not dilated, not irregular, no sign as of now of any trauma to the brain. Can't tell until the hospital X-Rays him. He's pale and clammy, in shock. Bleeding from a whack to the back of the head, also a little bump where he hit the floor. I'm hoping this is strictly a surface injury. You may see some considerable edema before this is over. Black and blue."

Together the two paramedics lifted Pete onto the stretcher. Marsha hovered close to him as they took him out into the ambulance. In a few minutes, the ambulance was speeding away with lights and sirens.

"What happened, Mr. Owens?" asked Deputy Toole, who held a pen and notepad ready.

Paul explained what little he knew. "...And we made the mistake of letting him go alone to get his model airplane."

"Do you know what the intruders were after?"

Just then there was a knock on the door. "Everybody be quiet." The door opened, and in walked a familiar figure. He was a tall, dark-haired man and he wore a red-brown-blue checkered flannel shirt, jeans with a cowboy belt, and deck shoes. Waving a billfold with badge and I.D., he introduced himself: "Special Agent John Mandigar, FBI. Mr. Owens and I are old friends."

"I'm the Principal Investigator," Toole said, introducing himself.

"Not any more. Sorry, but this is a top secret matter and your department will not be in the loop."

"I'll have to get the Sheriff on the phone."

"Washington already did that. He's on his way here to confirm to you what I'm saying." Mandigar turned to Paul. "What happened?"

"My neighbor's son was assaulted by a burglar."

"What were they after?"

"I don't know—and I don't know that you have the clearance or the need to know, since you're declaring this a federal gig."

"Still cheeky, huh?"

"This isn't the Soviet Union, Mandigar, and I'm going to ask you to keep a civil tongue in your rather square head."

Mandigar put his badge on his belt, accidentally revealing the rather large and ugly handle of a .38 cradled under his arm. "The woman your girlfriend?"

"Yeah." Mandigar was sure to know all about it, so why resist?

"I see you're upset. That's okay. You keep a civil tongue, and so will I. Deal?" He looked Paul up and down with an ugly grin.

"Okay. So which one of you is going to solve the crime, after the small talk is over?"

"Mr. Owens, answer me one question. Be aware that your ass may be right back in the frying pan if you lie, prevaricate, or otherwise screw around with me."

"There goes the civil tongue. Oh, I'm sorry, you don't have one, no wonder you can't stop insulting me, you verbal diarrhea machine."

"I'll wait outside," Toole said.

"Owens, did you bring work home?"

"No."

"Then what are they after?"

"I don't know."

"Bullshit." Mandigar pulled up a chair, turned it around, and straddled it with his arms folded on the back. "An absent minded professor like you is likely to pick up some top secret document and walk to his car, reading it, and drive all the way home, miraculously not getting in a car wreck while he continues reading. I've been on this beat for ten years, Owens, and I've seen it all."

"I have never brought anything classified home. Not even absorption test samples."

Mandigar waved a finger. "No, no, what I just heard was that you never brought anything classified home. So what did you bring home that wasn't classified that someone would be after."

"The boy's going to live, Mandigar," Paul said.

"I heard the damn ambulance jockey, Owens. I'm not deaf. I'm rejoicing inwardly. My problem is that I don't know what you eggheads are cooking up in that loony bin over there, but I do know I've been told to give my life if necessary to save you guys for America. That's asking a lot of me, and that's why I appear pissed off a lot of the time. I'm not interested in throwing my life away for you, Owens, and I don't like having to jump off the couch in the middle of the night to run to your house. Now what were they after?"

"Who?" Paul pressed back. He gripped the back of Mandigar's chair and shook it. "Who is after what?"

"Could be three things. A plain burglar. A Soviet spy. Or—."

"Or?"

"—Sometimes we get mercenaries. Those are Americans, usually, who'll steal anything they can and sell it to whoever offers top dollar. Once in a while, guys like that latch up with Soviet agents, who are after something. Now what would they be after?" Mandigar rose and walked around the room with his arms spread. "What's missing, Owens? Goddamn it, stop playing games and start looking."

Paul looked at the table. "The model airplane." He hurried to the table, looked beside it, under it. "It's gone! Pete's model airplane!"

"Model airplane?"

"Yes. It's just a flying saucer a little boy and I made. But—.."

There was a knock on the door. Paul said: "Yes?"

Steve Rossi and Ben Rich stood outside. "We came as fast as we could. What's going on here?"

Paul said: "I'm beginning to put together a picture of what happened."

Mandigar said: "Yeah, so am I. Owens, ..." He shut up and shook his head.

Paul explained: "I think these were the same people who searched my place a couple of weeks ago. I thought it was you, Mandigar, in your zeal to prove I'm a Commie or something."

"I do remember you babbling about that."

"It wasn't you. It was someone who knew that I was working on something highly sensitive. It wasn't a secret yet, and it was just in my head, but someone was on to me."

Rossi said: "Mr. Mandigar, if I may explain. I think I may have unwittingly added to this. You see, when Paul handed us his model for a top secret project, we tested it and found he's absolutely right. It's very important. I was so excited that I called him in the middle of the night. He was under pressure from the auditors and from you, and I knew it would be a great relief to him to know he was on the right track. I think I also admonished him not to talk about it. I may have said something like "this is now a highly classified project.' I—I—could kick myself for being so careless."

Ben said: "Oh boy. I'll have to dance around that like a ballerina. Paul, did you ever bring any secret materials home?"

"Never."

"Then what—?"

"The model," Paul said. "You guys stripped off the mockup itself and gave me back the chassis. I then built a flying saucer for the little boy next door. Pete must have surprised the intruder, and the intruder hit him over the head. The flying saucer is gone."

"How is the boy?" Ben asked.

"He's getting X-Rays. He was breathing and in shock when they wheeled him out of here."

"Mrs. Kassner's boy?"

"Yes."

"I'm sorry that poor woman's going through hell."

Paul noticed that the Sheriff's squad car rolled to a stop outside. So did another police car to keep traffic moving through the forest of flashing lights. Paul saw Jeff Toole in an animated conversation. Or rather, the Sheriff, an older, potbellied man with wiry gray hair, did most of the talking, and Toole mostly nodded.

"Where are you going to look for the intruders?" Paul asked Mandigar.

Mandigar sighed deeply. "I'm not sure."

Ben said: "If I may make a suggestion—they have a harmless flying saucer? Why don't we let them keep it?"

Steve added: "Good point. If we do nothing, then it will confirm their results when they bring this thing to Moscow—it's a dud."

Mandigar nodded. "Good. I like it. I do want to find out who they are so that we can watch them while they don't know we'll be watching them."

"Deal," Ben said. He turned to Paul. "Terrible thing about the child. I'll go over to the hospital and see how they're doing. Want to come?"

Paul thought about it. Pete had been brutally beaten, and nothing was going to happen? He said: "There is just one stop I'd like to make. It might help you verify who your suspects are. Then we'll all be happy, okay?"

"Explain."

"I'll explain on the way." To Ben he said: "I'll need one thing from you, even if you have to drive to the plant right now and get it."

"Sure," Ben said. "What is it?"

Chapter 27.

While he waited for Ben to call from the plant, Paul called the hospital. After some confusion, he reached the E.R. and Marsha came on the phone. "Yes?" Her voice was a shaky whisper.

"It's Paul. How is Pete?"

"He has a concussion. They just rushed him through X-Ray and there's no skull fracture or anything. No sign of trauma to the brain. Just a hugely ugly swelling on the back of his head. He's sleeping now. I guess we'll spend the night here."

"I'll be up to see you, but I'm working with the police on this, and there's a little something I have to take care of."

Around midnight, Paul was in the passenger seat of the FBI cruiser.

Mandigar drove. "Maybe your real calling in life was to be a cop. You might just be on to something, Owens."

"I hope so. It would kind of dot the i's and cross the t's a bit."

"It would tie things up pretty neatly for me if your hunch is correct. Sorry I've been a dick."

"It's your job."

"I'm a dick all the time."

"Okay, so you're on the job all the time."

"Without the hair, you're not so bad."

"Can we have a little variation in our society?"

Mandigar didn't reply. Maybe the idea of individual freedoms was pushing it a bit too far for him, Paul thought, but he gave the guy credit for trying despite a bad upbringing. After a 40 minute drive, they pulled off the freeway into a well-to-do Los Angeles suburb.

"So," Mandigar said. "If you're right, we should be able to push a few buttons and watch your toy fly around, and that will tell us exactly where to raid if that's what we want to do." He looked in some papers. "Hey, the guy who owns the house here is someone named Alex Fitch. Now why does that ring a bell?"

"Speaking of dicks," Paul said. "Just hover around the corner. Don't drive by, not even once. This place may be cold as ice, but if it is hot, it will be red hot."

"I agree," Mandigar said, turning off the engine. He rolled down the windows automatically, and cool night air filled the car. "Don't see anybody."

Paul looked diagonally across the street, down the block, and thoroughly hated the quaint red-brick colonial style home there, with its manicured lawn and green Jaguar in the driveway. He could have asked Marsha, but he didn't want to upset her—because it was a wild hunch anyway.

"Look," Paul said suddenly, spotting another car. "That big black square looking car? I think that's the car that the two guys were driving the first time I was burglarized." He reached into the back seat and pulled out the control box for Condor III. He licked his lips nervously and applied sweaty fingers to the controls, just barely touching them, while they were still off. "This is only a wild card."

"I know, I know," Mandigar said, eyeing the toy. "But it's worth the effort. I'm intrigued. What the hell you guys from that plant don't do with your goddamn time, I'll never understand."

A light went on in the house, spilling yellow shine onto the lawn.

It was very quiet in the house. No raucous laughter.

Aw hell, Paul thought, I'm making a fool out of myself.

"We are going to be noticed if we sit here too long," Mandigar said.

Then Mandigar gripped Paul's arm. "Listen."

They heard the swish of a car, and sure enough, another mean-looking black sedan pulled into the driveway. Three men got out and knocked on the door. Alex Fitch, wearing dark clothes, admitted them and quickly closed the door.

"If my guess is right," Paul said, "he'll have it sitting on the living room table or something."

"Don't try to recover it. Make the kid another one. I want to track these clowns."

"No problem. You ready?"

In answer, Mandigar started the engine. He left the lights off. The big car had a quiet, whispering engine.

"Here goes." Paul took a deep breath.

There was enough light for him to see the controls in the panel clearly.

He made fists, wiggled his fingers, then set his hands to the task.

First he turned on the power.

"Jesus," Mandigar said, "you hear that?"

They heard a sound like three tiny lawnmowers.

"Quick now," Paul said to himself. He pressed the hover bar up, and he estimated that the saucer would now be about three feet in the air. He upped it, in case it was on the floor.

They heard a muffled shout.

Paul feathered the 3% differential on the left rear engine. "Wherever it is, it should be spinning around the room in circles now."

They heard more shouts.

Paul saw the saucer bump against the window.

Great. There it was.

He knew what to do.

First he backed it away from the window.

Then he ran it toward the window again.

"Screw it, enough," Mandigar said. "We've got what we need. Let's not blow it."

The saucer came crashing through the window in a shower of glass.

Paul cut the power and the saucer dropped with a clatter.

The door opened, and Fitch came running out, a figure of desperate confusion.

Paul made fists and laughed triumphantly. Then he remembered Pete, and his malevolent wishes toward Fitch dissolved in a cloud of regret.

Mandigar, dour as ever, backed the car down the street quietly for several blocks, flying along at thirty or forty miles per hour, to an intersection, where he let the car back up in a Y turn, then put it in Forward and accelerated down the street.

"Thanks," Mandigar said as they cruised along the freeway back to Burbank. "One of these days I'm going to bust that guy hard. But first we'll find out who all his pals are. Might be quite a catch a year or two down the road."

Paul thought: And the Soviets will lose a year at least, or maybe they'll just ignore Ufimtsev even more thoroughly.

After Mandigar dropped him off, Paul called the hospital.

A night clerk answered and told Paul that Marsha was fast asleep in a cot next to Pete's bed—and that Pete was doing better. Paul asked the clerk to leave a note for Marsha to call him at home. He called the plant and left a note with the night guard that he would be in late tomorrow.

Then he swigged down two beers to calm his nerves, and fell asleep fully dressed lying on his back on the living room couch.

A repeated knocking noise woke Paul.

He groaned and sat up, blinded by shaft of sunlight that had been attempting to bore a hot hole through his forehead for at least twenty minutes.

"Paul!"

Hearing Marsha's voice, he stumbled through the kitchen. She stood at the back door, looking very girl next door in a long print dress and tennies. Her long dark hair was tied back in a pony tail, giving her face a pert look.

He opened the door and she hugged him.

"How's Pete?" He stroked her neck, her back, ran his fingers through over her hair.

"He's sleeping. He's okay, but I don't want to leave him alone for a second. Want to come over and visit?"

"Yes. Let me splash some water on my face, shave, shower..."

She drew imaginary figures on his T-shirt, over his heart. "Why don't you bring your things and do that... a little later? I have designs on you."

"Oh. You bet."

She hurried back to her house, looking nervously left and right, as if more violent felons were about to pop out of the shadows and harm her son. Paul shook his head, realizing last night's events had not helped his cause with her.

He washed up and strode across the lawn.

She was in the kitchen, fixing something to eat, and looked up with a little cloud of confusion. "Didn't you bring your shaving things?"

He laughed. "Honey, I live next door. It's not like I have to drive ten miles to my house."

She laughed and made a blowing motion, tossing some loose hair up over her forehead. "I see. That makes sense. I'm making you some breakfast."

He went to her, stood behind her, wrapped his arms around her as she fussed by the stove. He pulled her to him, and she complied, fitting her body to his as if they had been molded together, made for one another. She murmured: "Are you hungrier for food or for me?"

"You," he said into her ear.

She giggled. "Your breath tickles." She turned and put her arms around his neck. Her lips rose to meet his, and his heart beat faster as he immersed himself in a long kiss. His hands roved down her body, encountering only the thin material of her long dress. She was wearing absolutely nothing underneath. She sensed his quickening breathing and whispered in his ear, so that her breath was hot and moist: "I wanted to surprise you."

No more words. They walked hand in hand to the bedroom at the other end of the house and closed the door. She was more passionate than she'd ever been.

It was a timeless hour, though she tiptoed out after their second lovemaking to check on Pete, who was locked in his bedroom—and she carried the key. Paul realized later he should have seen the tip-off. But he didn't. She returned to the master bedroom and climbed on top of him, lifting her dress as she did, arranging her knees on either side of him, pressing him with her firm thighs as she seated herself and began to rock. He could only writhe with pleasure.

Exhausted, they lay lazily together in a brine of afternoon sunlight.

"I could go on and on like that forever," he said as they lay entwined.

She stroked his hair and smiled. Her eyes looked big and dark and moist and full of affection and humor.

"I'm going to make a new Condor for Pete and send it up to you."

"That would be nice." She touched his nose with her fingertip.

"Maybe you'll come to visit—."

She put her hand over his mouth. "Let's not talk at all about that today." She pulled him closer to her and soon they were dozing drowsily.

The phone rang, waking them up. Marsha answered and then

handed the phone to Paul. It was Steve Rossi. "How are you doing?"

Paul did not even want to guess how Steve had figured out where to reach him. "I think we're all doing fine now."

Marsha tiptoed back out, key in hand, to see Pete.

"Good job last night. Hey, take the day off."

"I was going to come in for a while this afternoon."

"You deserve a break. Come in early in the morning and we'll have a meeting with Ben. We have a lot of exciting stuff coming up."

Paul thanked him and they rang off.

Marsha came back with Pete, who stumbled sleepily. His eyes had slight shiners, and there was a bandage wrapped around his head.

"You poor fellow," Paul said, kneeling down. He held out his arms and Pete embraced him, still grunting sleepily.

"Thanks," Pete said.

"That was a scary business," Paul said.

"Yeah. And my saucer is gone."

"I'm gonna make you a newer and better one this month. We'll call it Condor IV. How's that?"

Pete smiled. "Yeah. That will be okay. We leave Sunday and—."

Marsha interrupted. "That will be enough, Peter. We agreed to not talk about that at all for today. Sunday is still almost a week away, so let's not spoil our time together."

"Okay, Mom."

"Paul, I'm going to throw your eggs out and start over. They're cold."

"Your eggs are hot," he whispered in her ear.

She nudged him away with her hip. "Stop it."

After their early supper, they went to see a funny family movie. Marsha held Paul tightly with her arm around his and her shoulder pressed against his. Pete sat on the other side of Paul. This must be what being married was like, Paul thought, glowing inside, though the glow had that distant rim of approaching loss and pain.

That night, Marsha was more ardent than ever.

Chapter 28.

In the morning Paul walked briskly into the plant and to Ben's office. Steve and Bill Schroeder were already there. They all shook hands. Several more engineers filed in. Ben asked about Pete, then broke into his opening salvo: "Gentlemen, I have great news. I've just learned that we and Northrop have won the first phase of the competition for the huge stealth contract. What we have to do now is to get ready for the next step, which is a clash of prototypes under field test conditions. We and Northrop have each been awarded a million and a half dollars to develop the prototypes."

"I want to take this opportunity to thank Bill Schroeder, who came out of retirement to help us with the Echo I project." He shook Bill's hand, and there was a round of applause from the small group.

"Back to the hearth fire," Bill quipped.

Each man shook Bill's hand.

"We now have a new project name with our one and a half million bucks," Ben said. "Our internal project name is Hopeless Diamond, and we're in direct competition with Northrop. We need to have a model the Air Force refers to as an Experimental Survivable Testbed or XST, meaning the model does not get destroyed during testing. Our first job will be putting the specifications together, but we know it will be around 40 feet long, so that should give you an idea. Our model, and Northrop's, will be stuck on a pylon at White Sands Range for competitive testing. Whoever wins gets one heck of a hefty contract. I want that contract, gentlemen, and I'm going to give everything I've got to nail it down."

Paul nodded as Ben's gaze fiercely made the rounds of his core group. It was Ben's third project as director of the Skunk Works. He'd done great on the first two, but this project, because of its outlandishness, was considered both a risk and a challenge for him. He still had Kelly Johnson looking over his shoulder a bit, but no amount of mentoring could save Ben if this thing went down in flames—not only were huge sums of money involved, but the Skunk Works' reputation was on the line.

"First thing we need to do," Ben said, "is to grow this thing through a series of subscale models until we arrive at the full blown configuration at about 47 feet. We only have a few months to get to White Sands, gentlemen, so let's make every minute count."

There was a murmur of assent as the men rose, for the meeting was over.

Paul walked Bill Schroeder to his car and thanked him for his great support. They shook hands, and Bill drove off, looking a bit misty.

Paul returned to his lab. He still hadn't had time to unpack, and it looked as if there wouldn't be for some time. He made a mental note to return to Mr. Garcia's metal shop with a new design for Condor IV. He glanced at the wall clock. It was 10:45. He picked up the phone and called Marsha.

No answer.

Probably out shopping. Funny, come to think of it, she hadn't mentioned anything about his coming over for lunch, which they'd been doing every day since her breakup with Fitch.

Paul stood back as a message cart arrived, bearing several rolled up blueprints—the first specs for the subscale 25 foot model, still hot from the drafting room's plotter press. Paul unrolled the documents, placed metal weights on each corner, and began poring over the detailed measurements. He found two small errors right off, which he noted by circling them with a red china marker.

He was still going over the first drawing, when he noted a hunger pang. He picked up the phone and called Marsha again.

No answer.

Grabbing his sweater, he walked out the door.

He felt more than a little hunger pang.

He got in his car and drove out of the parking lot.

He drove along the roads into Madeira, curious that their constant chain of contact over the past few weeks seemed to be broken at the moment.

He gasped as he approached his house. A small moving van stood parked in front of Marsha's house, with the garage door open. The realty sign had been taken down when the house went into escrow. This could not be someone moving in. The truck was too small, and the four men milling about her garage could not be the family that was buying.

Her car was gone.

What is going on? He parked in his driveway and got out in a daze.

He noticed the letter stuck in his front door screen, but in his shock, he walked over to her house.

The doors were tightly locked, the windows shuttered.

"Hello," he said, approaching the four men in blue overalls who were emptying her garage of everything that wasn't nailed down.

"Hi," said their leader, an older man with white hair. He showed Paul a memorandum from the Veterans of Foreign Wars. Mrs. Kassner was permitting them to take away all the possessions she was placing for them in the garage—

Paul jogged to his own door. He pulled the letter out, sat down hard, and peeled it open. He swallowed hard as he read, in her neat, precise penmanship:

"Dearest Paul, I'm sorry to bail out this way, but it's maybe the easiest for both of us. I am afraid to spend another night in this town with Peter after what just happened. Also, I care greatly about you, and I don't want to continue our relationship. This is not because of you, because you are a wonderful man, but I don't feel about you the way I felt about Jeffrey. I have been making a series of mistakes lately, and I don't want to make another one with you. I don't think I love you in that way, and I don't want to hurt you any more than I am doing today. I am looking forward to living back in Oregon, and I want to just make a new life for me and my son there. I want you to continue in your wonderful job, because I know you love it. Please let me go. I'm sorry to hurt you, and I wish you all the best. Sincerely, Marsha Kassner."

Paul slowly laid the letter down on the ground between his feet, where a light wind moved it about.

He planted his elbows on his knees and sank his face into his palms.

Suddenly, he found himself crying uncontrollably.

Blindly, with his face on fire and hurting from the salty sting and the insult to his mucus tissues, he unlocked the door and went inside to avoid the curious gaze of the four VFW workers.

He put on a kettle of water for tea. Listening to the kettle banging, he tried to catch the loosely spinning newsreel of his thoughts, but he felt as if he'd been smashed with a hammer. His hands trembled, and he sniffled uncontrollably for at least ten minutes. During that time he looked first out the east window at her house, now an abandoned and lifeless shell, then out the south window over the sink, at his now desolate radar emulation, where Pete had danced happily with the

Condor planes for many hours.

When the kettle started to whistle, he turned it off.

He washed his face in hot water at the sink, breathing shallowly to relieve the reddened channels of his nose. His eyes felt as if they'd doubled in size and were full of peperoncini juice. He dabbed them gently with a clean, dry kitchen towel.

He dropped a tea bag in the cup, filled it with steaming water, added some honey, and went outside to sit on the back porch. If he was still hungry, he didn't feel it anymore. Clouds were moving in, and the yard looked as desolate as he felt.

After a while, he put his empty teacup in the sink. As he locked up the house, he noted the men and the van were gone, and it was all over. He drove back to work.

There, he bought a dry sandwich—baloney with cheese—from a vending machine as he walked through the plant. He bought a hot cup of acid coffee from another machine and carried these to his lab. It was going to be a long couple of months pushing out those prototypes, and he didn't plan to spend much of that time at home. He'd get over this because he'd always been a survivor, he knew, and this had really only been a fling of a few weeks, and hell, he'd spent much of that feeling bad as she traipsed around with dear old Alex Fitch. Maybe by Spring time, he thought, he'd be feeling a little better, maybe take a little time off and meet someone. Right now, he couldn't think of anything but Hopeless Diamond, and the wall of numbness looming all around him. Already, he was flexing some inner muscles to push that wall away. She was actually right, he thought; he deserved better than he'd gotten...and so he resolved to leave her be and push on with his life.

Chapter 29.

At one end of the plant was a room, which Ben had converted into an anechoic chamber, meaning that its walls were almost perfectly radar absorbent. The walls, floor, and ceiling were lined with rows of sharply pointed metal studs arranged in rows; any stray electromagnetic signals would scatter among the hundreds of studs and be absorbed by the surfaces behind the studs.

Paul and Steve supervised as the 25 foot next-step-up subscale model took shape outside the anechoic chamber. Already, in the smooth plywood model, the mixed beauty and ugliness of the aircraft were becoming apparent.

"You either love this baby or you hate it," said Dick Scherrer, who was in charge of the initial design work, laying out the overall shape. Paul was beside him, checking out a measurement.

At his side laughed Ed "Baldy" Baldwin, who would have responsibility for moving the optimized shape onto a workable airframe. Baldy had been with the company since at least 1945, when he and Kelly had worked on the first U.S. jet fighter, the P-80. "Yeah," Baldy said, running a hand dubiously along the model's sharp edge. "This one is going to be one hell of a challenge." Baldy was known for his temperament. As of yet, he was still of pleasant mien. "I gotta make this thing fly, huh?"

"You could make a brick fly," Paul said, climbing around among electrical cables that made a spaghetti at the foot of the model.

Chapter 30.

Within a few months, the Skunk Works was ready to face its only remaining competitor, Northrop, in a set of field tests.

The winner would receive the award to build two full-size prototype stealth jets. That contract would be worth upwards of $28 million, as Ben Rich confided to his management team at a meeting.

Paul had almost no time to work on Condor IV, but he'd made Pete a promise. With Steve's understanding and permission, he drafted up a design one morning and handed it to a senior technician in the models shop. Paul provided three brand-new midsize model propellers. They turned out a delightful three engine saucer with a safety grill on the bottom so Pete wouldn't get his fingers mangled. A lid in the top opened so the operator could refill the three fuel cells. The shop got some delight out of the model, which Paul flew for them. One of them, an avid model airplaner, professionally spray painted the saucer in Air Force olive drab matte, and added a few catchy decals, including the words U.S. Air Force and an official looking star, all in miniature.

Steve's comment as he saw Paul going out for lunch was: "Maybe we should send another one of those to Moscow."

Paul wrapped the saucer in a plain bag to avoid attention. He wrote a small note to Pete and Marsha, pleasant but avoiding any signs of emotion. He bought a sturdy kit including a box and packing straw at a stationer's. He packed the saucer and the note and realized at the last minute he didn't know her address. Instead, he mailed it to her at her former address next door—it would be forwarded by the Postal Service, and he was done.

Done.

During the afternoon, Paul met with Baldy to take a preliminary look at some of the issues that would involve making the new design airworthy.

"This is the first aircraft designed by mathematicians," Baldy told him. "Couldn't you have started with the airframe and worked your way back to stealth?"

Paul shook his head. "No. This technology is stealthy on its own terms. We can predict from any point of view what a radar signal is going to return, and that's a signal the size of a ball bearing, no matter how big the plane is."

Baldy whistled appreciatively. "That would save pilots' lives, wouldn't it."

"Yes."

"I'm gonna work on it as hard as I can."

Ben stopped by just then, and looked over their shoulders.

"Look here." Baldy sifted through a layered topographic mound of blueprints. "The beauty of this is that we're not going to design a new plane from scratch. Since we've got the configuration handed to us on a platter, we might as well go out and see what we can take off the shelf. I'm looking at maybe putting this together here..." he flipped from one design to another, all blueprints that he was acquiring from various programs in Lockheed's inventory or anywhere else for that matter...like we can use those General Electric J-85-GE-4A engines from the T-2B Buckeye Trainer."

Ben interrupted: "Baldy, remember that all openings and surfaces have to withstand the radar test. No flat surface or straight line must ever be perpendicular to the sender of the radar signal."

"I gotcha covered, Ben. Look here." Baldy pulled out a sketch he'd made of two crazily zigzagging lines. "That's what I'm gonna try for the fit on the cockpit shell edges. We don't want any straight lines, so we break them up like I've done here."

"What do you think, Paul?" Ben asked.

"Looks good to me. Let's be sure and test all these concepts as early as possible."

"Great point," Ben said. "That's the purpose of gradually staged mockups—so we can design the problems out while the mockup is small. Good work, guys!" Ben left.

Baldy continued his recitation. "On those J-85's we've got to eliminate exhaust heat that could show up on radar or even infrared and get the pilot a heat-seeking missile up his tailpipe. The good thing here is that we can go subsonic, which makes a lot of things easier. She'll be painted a good mix of VLO (very low observable) colors. She'd fly only at night. The engines have got to be fairly quiet."

"What about stability?" Paul asked. "Aren't the engineers going nuts over the fact that this plane is liable to start doing curly-cues in the air and then crash?"

"Lucky thing computer technology is that far along," Baldy said. "We're going to design in an FBW, or Fly By Wire system, quadruple redundant to make sure there's backup. It's called a Relaxed Static Stability design, in which there are computer directed wires that lead to all the control surfaces. The computer figures out the wind factors— resistance, temp, and so forth—and keeps adjusting each point in the control system from second to second to keep her flying steady."

As he continued, Baldy pulled out one drawing after another, from various manufacturers and for various aircraft.

"We're shooting for a simple design—a modified delta with a tight sweep of about 72.5 degrees. No flaps, speed brakes, or high lift devices. We'll borrow a side-stick controller from the F-16. There is an interesting Lear-Seigler FBW command and stability augmentation system in the F-16 that I have my eye on. We'll use elevon nose-down pitch control inboard on the wings, and we'll put two moveable fins on top of the wing root, kind of canted inboard a bit. I don't now how sharply yet. We'll add a two-position flap that pulls it back in line when she goes beyond 12 per cent out of horizontal."

Paul said: "Everything has to be broken up so that nothing shows on radar."

"Got you. This plane is going to look like a spaceship."

"We'll have to continue working with Dick Scherrer on the models, and we'll have to test every line and surface to make sure it's optimized."

Baldy made a dour face. "Young fella, let me tell you something. More than one time over the past thirty years, I've seen a good clean design come from some young genius's drafting table, like yours here, and by the time the Air Force or the Navy are done telling us they need more bomb carrying capabilities, or more range, or more of this or more of that, the design was so fouled up it could make a grown man cry."

Paul felt puzzled by this line of comment.

"What I'm telling you, Paul, is that it's a long way from here to a successful working plane. And that's assuming we get the contract. Northrop is a big powerful company, and we're just this little pimple on Lockheed's butt. You see here that I'm knocking myself out to think all these little parts into it, but no design is going to be as perfect as your mathematical model. In the end, she may not be as stealthy as we thought. Or we may not even get the contract."

Paul had a wry feeling about that. "Baldy, life itself is unpredictable. I'm just focused on this from one step to the next."

Inwardly, all the self-doubts about the risks involved in this unorthodox concept began to nag at him. Ben seemed unflappable, but what was going on underneath the surface?

For over two months, Paul worked 14 and 16 hours, dragging himself home just to sleep exhaustedly and then return not long after dawn to start a new day.

Chapter 31.

As a warm-up for the real thing, Ben and Steve wanted to test a ten-foot wooden model of the Hopeless Diamond on an outdoor test range near Palmdale, on the Mojave Desert.

The range belonged to competitor McDonnell Douglas, and Lockheed made an arrangement to use their facility for a day or two.

As always, strict security had to be observed. For one thing, the Hopeless Diamond must never be visible to Soviet satellites that prowled in orbit above, devouring eye detail of any kind.

The ten-foot model was too long to fit into a standard van, and so Steve had to requisition a U-Haul van and a tower of blankets. Paul stressed over and over to everyone who'd listen that it was worth getting the largest transport vehicle available, to leave room for plenty of padding. The mockup must not be scratched or dented in any fashion or it would be a waste of time to take it to the range. The model was lifted by hand by a dozen technicians, carefully, slowly, onto a bed of blankets prepared in the van. It was covered with blankets, one blanket at a time, each blanket rolled so that its edges could not mar the matte black composite finish on the surfaces. Technicians then filled empty floor space around the model with cardboard boxes stuffed with styro packing peanuts.

Paul and Steve worriedly lowered the tailgate of the truck and made sure it was tightly locked.

"We'll have to drive real carefully to avoid getting in an accident," one of the engineers said.

Steve lit a cigarette and shrugged. "Buddy, at some time you gotta let go and hope for the best. We could worry this thing to the point that we fail for worrying."

Paul said: "I do want the truck parked under cover. I don't want it to sit there and bake in the desert heat because I'm afraid the wood might dry further and the paint might crack."

"Good point," Steve said. "You know, I think we can get the Air Force to provide us with one of those big camouflage nets that they drape over planes."

"Okay, I think we're ready to roll," Ben said. He tapped the back of the van, and the technician driving waved.

"I'll ride with him," Paul volunteered.

Ben grinned. "You're more nervous than I am."

"You better believe it."

It was a long, tedious, and enervating ride for Steve. The driver did not volunteer much conversation, and Paul in any case wanted him to concentrate on his driving. Their one luxury was that the driver chose a country western station that played softly much of the way to Palmdale, about three hours northeast of Los Angeles.

They arrived on the range around noon. Ben and Steve and the others had flown up in a DeHavilland Twin Otter from Burbank Airport and were waiting at the test pylon when Paul and his companion drove the van up, after getting lost twice and bumping around on side roads at five miles per hour. Once there was a thump from the back that had Paul ready to claw his way through the metal wall to check the model's condition.

The pylon already had a camouflage net draped over poles, so that it was invisible from the air. Steve waved for the driver to back the van up close to the pylon under the net.

Paul was the first on board to peel the blankets back. He breathed a sigh of relief. Not a mar or scratch in sight.

Gingerly, a group of eight men pulled the model out, including Ben and Steve and four Air Force technicians.

"Let's not put it down," Ben said as the model's tail section hung partially out over the concrete floor. "Let's do a smooth lift, walk about eight steps, and place the hole at the bottom of the model right onto the pylon. We must not drag the underbelly over the point, or it will be damaged. Got that?"

After a short rest, they said "one, two, three, lift" and wrested the heavy pound load through the air, then down, down, gingerly, gently, and it fit perfectly onto the pylon with a mere sigh of air escaping.

After an exchange of signals between the Air Force techs, there was a hydraulic whirr as the pylon rose up into its full 12 foot height.

"Looks beautiful," Steve said. "Looks like she's flying already."

"Good work!" Ben said. He asked the Air Force officer in charge, a young blond lieutenant with sunglasses, "Can we do this today?"

"Oh, absolutely, Sir. We can start right now if you wish."

Ben nodded. "Let's do it and see how it goes." He gave Paul a wink and crossed his fingers. Paul answered with a thumbs up, but his stomach was in butterflies.

"This is just our private Skunk Works test to rehearse for the real thing," Ben reminded everyone.

The lieutenant spoke by portable radio with the operator in a small building about 1500 feet away. A white radar dish turned slowly and aimed at the Hopeless Diamond.

The lieutenant spoke into the radio and gave a wave up-range. "Go!"

Paul, Ben, and Steve turned pale and hung on in the light desert breeze as one could have heard a cactus needle fall.

The lieutenant said to Ben: "There is something wrong, Sir. He's not getting any return at all."

Ben got a crafty expression on his face. He pointed gently at the Hopeless Diamond and said: "It can't be our model—she's right there."

The lieutenant seemed distressed. "I'm really sorry, Sir. I hope we're not having trouble with our megatron." He spoke into the radio again. "What do you mean it's on max? You're not seeing a thing? Not even at full power?"

Just then, a crow flew by. Losing its way slightly, it landing slowly, flapping its wings, on top of the mockup.

The lieutenant brightened. "Okay, Sir, it's working. He's getting a nice fat signal."

Ben cleared his throat and looked utterly innocent.

Steve's eyes burned in silent triumph, while his facial muscles rippled at the effort he was making to restrain loud laughter and howling.

Paul ran over and clapped his hands.

The crow flew away, leaving a deposit.

The lieutenant started looking baffled again.

Ben whispered: "When we get back, I'm buying."

Chapter 32.

In March 1976, the full-sized mockup of Hopeless Diamond was ready to ship to Rat Scat Test Range at White Sands, New Mexico for its do or die competition with whatever Northrop was putting forth. Rumor in the industry was that Northrop's powerful combination of structural and coating elements would be unbeatable.

In a meeting the day before shipping, Paul reminded Ben: "Everything hangs on the fact that nothing must touch the model's surfaces. We cannot afford even a tiny ding on the leading wing edge, or a bird dropping on the fuselage. Even a fly sitting on the cockpit window could give back a return, with the 50,000-watt megatron radar source they are going to use."

"I hear you," Ben said. "It's going to require every ounce of our attention. I want you watch their every move."

"I wouldn't do it any other way," Paul said.

Ben confided: "Rumor has it Northrop has an extremely sophisticated design with some faceting and some rounded corners, and the most advanced composites and paints imaginable."

Paul felt a sine wave of sheer icy terror pass through his gut. Rounded? Could that mean Northrop had leapfrogged over the computer problem and actually programmed a design with curved surfaces—more complex polygons than just the triangles the Hopeless Diamond was using?

Ben saw the look on Paul's face and said darkly: "I can almost hear the laughter out there. We've come this far, old buddy, we might as well go in swinging."

It was one of the only times that Paul saw a twinge of doubt on Ben's face. And why not? This design looked so strange that it was hard to be cheered for long over the incident with the crow. What if there had indeed been a short or something? What if the crow had in reality had nothing to do with the failed return? And the Skunk Works did not have a 50,000-watt megatron like White Sands, or even a 25,000-watt device like that at Palmdale. Most of the testing had been done with weaker radars. Oh Jeez, Paul thought, I feel like wetting my pants. Too late now for any further design mods.

The next morning a huge flatbed truck arrived, contracted from a civilian firm, with an ugly but powerful gray cab to tow it along.

Once again, major security had to be enforced. The truck had to back up into the hangar. Now the problem was how to lift the 38-foot behemoth the size of a small yacht without damaging it. This time, it would take more than a dozen men.

The model sat on a steel cradle, protected by rubber bumpers on the steel struts. The full size Hopeless Diamond had been built of wood, all in flat panels cut to precision by the model making shop. All edges had been carefully buttered to be invisible to radar, using radar-absorbing iron ball paints. The Hopeless Diamond reminded some of Darth Vader's helmet, especially now that it had been painted matte black.

The steel cradle was parted as far as its wheeled exterior halves would go, and the flatbed sidled underneath. A pair of motorized overhead pulleys rolled along on their steel I-beam tracks—leftovers from a Korean War production line. Technicians wrapped blankets around the edges of the model, and loosely tied canvas straps around the model and then up over the pulley hooks.

The hooks tightened, and the model swayed in the air inches above the cradle.

The techs rolled the steel cradle away, and an operator lowered both pulleys evenly, very slowly, until the Hopeless Diamond sat snugly on its flatbed. Again it was wrapped in protective cushioning, and this time a canvas tent was laid over the steel poles in the edges of the flatbed, assuring the model was invisible to the air; and just as invisible to nosy fellow drivers on the road to White Sands, New Mexico. This time, two armed men from Lockheed's security branch would ride in the truck along with the driver, and Paul would fly to White Sands with Ben, Steve, and Kelly Johnson.

It would be a few days before they could fly there. The truck would have to drive to White Sands. Then Air Force technicians and security experts would take over. These tests meant potentially billions of dollars in funding, and everything had to be done in an atmosphere of 100% fairness and even-handedness. The powerful aerospace companies demanded and received precision attention. There would be no hands-on lifting of the models here. Air Force experts would handle every detail, from transporting the models to mounting them to testing them. The makers of the models would not be allowed to lay a hand on their creations during the official testing period to prevent tampering or cheating.

The evening before he flew to New Mexico, Paul found a letter in his mailbox. It was from Pete Kassner. He opened it with shaky fingers and read: "Dear Paul: Thanks very much for the wonderful saucer. I named it Condor IV in honor of you. It flies beautifully. Mom says hello. We miss you. Sincerely, Pete."

Paul stood in the doorway in the sunset and read the letter several times, trying to read between the lines. He was glad the boy was happy. *We miss you...* was that Pete talking, or both of them? If she wanted to, she would have called or written by now. Paul looked at the unused shelf high up near the door, where a plastic plant had been gathering dust in a fake pot since he'd moved in here three years ago. He supposed that Mrs. Garcia occasionally dusted there, but he never bothered. He reached up and felt around. There lay the note Marsha had written to him the day she'd bailed out. He slipped Pete's letter up to lie on top of that. He had no idea how he felt about them anymore. It had been several months without any contact. He resisted the urge to throw their notes away. He would walk away from this. He would let the notes lie there like leaves that have fallen off tries and slowly rot to nothing, so that a stray wind blows their brittle remains away.

Not long after Marsha's departure, new neighbors moved in. They were the Polanskis, a 40ish couple from Scranton, Pennsylvania, come here to start Madeira's first furniture store. Karl Polanski was a tall, thin man who moved with languid self-assurance. He was balding and had a devouring, intelligent gaze. Paul sat on the porch a few evenings, sharing a beer and political views with Polanski.

Dorothy Polanski was a small, robust graying woman with thick glasses. She had youthful skin, despite the gray hair, and it appeared she did not use much makeup. They had two children, both in high school. Beth was 16, a lovely dark-haired girl with a close, quiet manner. Her typical body language was to hold her school books to her chest with both arms and to stand slightly pigeon-toed. Aaron was 15 and a power soccer player, a fast runner, with a large bone structure and an aggressive chin. Paul could see the mix of features in them from their parents—Karl's incisive gaze, Dorothy's athletic plainness.

Dorothy was an excellent cook and they had Paul over for dinner two or three times. He felt odd, sitting in that same kitchen where... but it was a form of innoculation, he thought. One day he could look at that house or sit in that kitchen without remembering that a certain woman had once briefly lived there.

Life went on. The Polanskis were very much the reality now, not any of the many other people who'd lived under that roof in the 100 years of its existence.

Chapter 33.

White Sands was located just northeast of Las Cruces, New Mexico, which lay on the intersection of Interstates 10 running east-west and 25 running north-south.

The tests were scheduled to last about a month. Northrop's people would not get a look at Lockheed's, nor would Lockheed's people see what Northrop had to offer.

Paul, Ben, and Steve flew to Las Cruces in a Lear jet owned by Lockheed. They Lockheed stayed in a Howard Johnson's near White Sands, and the location of the Northrop team wasn't disclosed to them. These security measures worked both ways.

Ben had arranged for himself and his two co-workers to stay in Las Cruces the first two or three days, to return to Burbank, and then to spend the last two or three days at White Sands again.

As they rode in a taxi to the test range their first morning at White Sands, Steve sighed deeply. "Well, here we go. This is the whole enchilada."

Paul found himself laughing nervously. "I'll be glad when this is over because we'll know one way or the other."

Ben said quietly: "There will be other contracts. Each one of them is unique and exciting, if you think about it—the SR-71, the U-2, the D-21..." He added: "...Somehow I don't think any of them stacks up against the potential to change history of this one. Just think—planes will be able to fly invisibly through the enemy's radar and drop precision bombs right down his shirt collar. If we get the contract, gentlemen, we will change history."

Ben had been wise in scheduling a few days on the front end, Paul thought. Several funny situations came up that required Paul's close attention.

What a boring activity testing was, Paul thought as he looked around. Everywhere you went in New Mexico, it seemed, you were on perfectly flat desert or scrub land—always with purplish mountains in the distance. It was a beautiful country in a unique kind of way, he thought, very empty, scoured, as if there had been an ocean here and it had gone away. Which was actually the truth, he remembered from his reading in geology.

The test activities went forward at a slow, methodical pace. Air Force enlisted personnel did most of the lifting around here, and they were all very proficient, though there was a kind of pacing to it—there would be more of the same tomorrow, and the day after that, and the day after that, until one's enlistment was over, so why rush? The wind blowing in the sage brush at evening, and the dead brush rolling across a deserted street, and the silvery half moon pasted onto a perfect black sky squirming with millions of stars, all seemed to agree.

During the day the heat got up there, and the sky was a translucent blue with frequent contrails that quickly evaporated as their moisture was sucked up by the dry air.

The testing went in stages, and each stage had a Northrop half and a Lockheed half. The Skunk Works was up at bat at the top of the first inning, and Paul had a chance to work with the techs—though of course he was not allowed to touch the model.

The first day, there was a flap because something was wrong with the imaging. Paul stood by as a captain and a master sergeant—like all Air Force personnel around here clad in fatigues and combat boots—had a spirited discussion.

The NCO said: "Sir, we've got their model on the pylon, and the model doesn't show up, but the pylon is glowing like a night light."

The captain said: "Hmm. Are you aiming correctly? Checked your power?"

"Sir, I've run every check in the book. There is something wrong with our setup."

"Sergeant, I'll be happy to call base radar group. We can't stand here like this all day."

"I know, Sir, you're right, we have a full schedule. Maybe if we bring in a different magnetron?"

"Good idea. Call radar group and have them bring a different unit—one they know for sure is recertified and working properly."

"Yessir."

Paul went to a nearby roach coach and bought coffee and a donut. When he returned, Ben and Steve had returned from a visit to some base brass. "What's going on?" Ben asked."

Paul shrugged. "They think their radar isn't working."

"Any crows around?" Steve quipped.

"I was thinking that," Paul said. He pointed with his donut at the Hopeless Diamond, whose 38-foot silhouette looked majestic and soaring atop a tall pylon under a camouflage net. "They are going to replace their radar equipment. I'm going to wait."

"Yeah, don't say a thing," Ben said. "In fact, let's distance ourselves." They walked away about fifty feet.

A kind of tow motor or tractor arrived, moving slowly across the tarmac with a trailer in tow. On the trailer sat a large rectangular unit resembling a generator. A jeep with four technicians followed. Stenciled in black along the jeep's fenders a legend read: Radar Group A.

Paul had an idea of what was wrong. Sure enough, an hour later, after Group had swapped generators, the situation remained the same. The operators had a fit, holding their heads and walking around in circles. The captain appeared baffled.

"You'd better help them," Ben suggested.

Paul nodded. He walked over to the NCO. "Hello, Sarge. What's the trouble?"

The NCO, whose name tag read Marchant, shook his head. "We've never imaged our pylon before. It's strange—like a complete reversal. Before, we'd stick a test subject up there and shoot—and get the test subject; no pylon except maybe a faint smudge at about minus 20 decibels. Now we're seeing the pylon lit up like a Christmas tree, but no test subject."

Paul offered: "Can I make a suggestion? Take down the mockup and shoot the pylon. I think you'll get the same result."

The captain had heard this and stepped up somewhat heatedly. "What's the point? We don't have time to fool around here."

"It's not working," Paul reminded him. "I think the problem is that our radar signature is virtually zero. Before, you had objects with a signature big as a locomotive, and it drowned out the pylon. Our technology is so good that it makes your pylon look like flash bulbs going off."

The captain looked as if he'd swallowed a frog.

The NCO said: "I think you have a point there."

An hour later, a senior colonel told Ben Rich: "If you guys are so damned smart, why don't you build us a pylon that's as stealthy as you say your technology is."

Ben talked this over with Paul. "I don't see any harm in it. Northrop will see our new pylon but they won't be able to figure our technology. It's too late for them to steal anything. If we lose here, we lose. But if we win here, the world is ours."

"I'll design them a pylon," Paul said.

"I'd like you to stay here and honcho this whole business for me," Ben said. "Steve and I have to get back to Burbank, because we have a lot to do."

That afternoon, before leaving in the taxi with Steve, Ben told Paul: "I've worked out a deal with the Air Force, and they're working something out with Northrop. These tests are going to be meaningless unless the Air Force can quantify our radar signature within a tenth of a decibel. I threw out a quick and dirty estimate that a new pylon will cost $500,000."

"And the Air Force won't pay it," Steve added, one foot up on in the open door of the cab, ready to leave.

Ben said: "So Lockheed and Northrop will each pay half. They've agreed to let you develop the pylon right here in their labs, using whatever resources you need, and we'll help from Burbank."

"I'll need computer time down there," Paul said. He was warming up to the challenge. In a way, it was a blessed relief to have this take up his time, rather than face the agonizing tension of this do-or-die sudden death competition, plus the whole business of putting back together a personal life for himself, which had been on hold, and looming at the periphery of his consciousness.

"You'll get whatever you need," Ben promised. Then he and Steve were whisked away in a jeep across the tarmac to the airfield.

Paul sat up in the hotel room late into the night. The table was strewn with papers. He'd borrowed a slide rule and a pocket calculator, and a couple of pens and mechanical pencils.

The design should be able to comfortably hold a five ton weight—that was in the one page spec hammered out between Northrop's engineers and White Sands production range engineering. It must not sway in a wind up to 25 knots, nor must the angle of deflection in a 50-knot gale for a five ton weight be more than ten degrees.

Maybe he'd go for a double wedge pylon, he thought. Two wedges would be stable versus the ground, and along the top use the structural integrity of the model to gain some stiffness. He'd need Baldy or someone at the Skunk Works to work out the specs for the inner steel frame. They might have to get Bill Schroeder to come in for a few days to do the math and run the computer programs to figure out the most stealthy configuration of triangles or facets.

In the morning, Paul called Burbank and told them what he needed. Rather than talk on the phone, he send a set of hand-drawn impromptu designs by registered mail to Ben Rich.

Then he waited. He went to the base library and checked out some books on math and engineering. He also checked out a stack of paperback novels, for the moment making sure to avoid ones that might have too much romance in them—he was up for reading about war and history, but not the interactions between a man and a woman.

The sameness of the days added to the lingering uncertainty and the aching dread that he'd made a mistake somehow. But he managed to remember that he was usually a fairly self-assured man. The events of the past few months had thrown him sorely for a loop.

Within a week, the folks back in Burbank had finished their design work and air freighted a rolled up tube, registered mail, containing the plans. Paul reviewed them and sent back a memo authorizing the construction—his largest responsibility to date, because he was responsible for a half million dollars of work.

And this was nearly untested! They had done some very successful miniature testing on wooden models, but not a full scale mockup.

He signed it off, and sent the memo back to Ben, who would copy everyone involved including Northrop Corporation.

Then he waited again. Unlike the usual hurry up and wait, however, there were fires lit under various personalities in the chain of command, and the Commandant at White Sands was anxious to get his HST behind him.

A construction crew installed the pylon on an unused concrete pad near the old pylon. The crew also installed several wooden telephone poles in a semicircle, over which camouflage netting would be draped. The twin-wedge pylons were slightly over 50 feet tall, and, with the full scale mockup on top, would be an imposing monument to aviation.

While the concrete hardened, Air Force technicians began testing the pole, from their 50,000-watt magnetron dish and shed 1500 feet from the target.

Paul waited with trembling knees, pacing back and forth.

One technician said: "Man, there's something wrong here. I don't see the pylon."

"Shoot the old pylon," an NCO said.

Ten minutes later, the tech said: "Geez, Sarge, what an ugly sight. The old pylon looks like it's on fire under water."

"Shoot the new pylon."

"Okay." A few minutes later, the tech said: "There's a little blip here the size of a bumblebee."

Pause.

Paul's knees began to shake from a new reason: elation.

"Holy shit," the NCO said. "If they can do that with a frigging pole, imagine what they can do with their model."

Every day, Ben called at least once to find out the latest. Paul told him what he'd overheard that day. Ben was ecstatic.

The next day, Air Force technicians resumed the planned testing.

The Hopeless Diamond sat on its pylons like a boy's model science fiction rocket. The design, Paul thought, was rather pleasing in a startling way. The Hopeless Diamond might be an ugly duckling on the ground, but it would be a hawk in the air. He trusted Baldy and the other designers to engineer a brick that flew like an arrow, and sing at the same time.

In the initial tests, the model had a radar cross-section about the size of a golf ball. Paul could tell that the testers were impressed. A number of senior colonels and one or two generals showed up now and then to look at the design and nod. They were all pilots, from the look of them, and Paul imagined they were eyeballing a future plane that they might be flying. They came in twos and threes, in relays it looked like, and they did not look dejected when they left. Or was it that they were pleased with both test candidates and just waiting for one to edge the other out?

The heat, the birds, other environmental stresses sent the tests one way or the other.

Birds began leaving their signatures, and they significantly increased the radar return. Up to twelve birds at once decided that they too would like to fly this new gizmo, and came to inspect and leave their opinions. The radar cross section doubled from 1.5 decibels to 3 decibels before the mockup could be carefully washed clean by young enlisted men on ladders, with soft sponges and pails of warm water containing ordinary, mild dishwashing detergent that should not harm the paints.

The cross section came back down to 1.5.

Then the heat set in, during day after day of testing at various frequencies and ranges. The heat could actually bend the signal, so that it missed the target entirely or partially. On one reading, the signature was four decibels off in the minus direction, which was better than the Hopeless Diamond could do.

Paul considered the implications and said nothing. No sense helping Northrop—they were probably experiencing the same effects. If the technicians did not catch their own errors, so be it—unless, of course, it went against Lockheed's favor. But it didn't.

Ben called every day on a secure line, and Paul filled him in.

"How big are the cross-sections," he would ask.

"As small as an eagle's eyeball," Paul would say.

Then one day, Paul said: "The size of a small ball bearing."

Ben was very excited. "Can you get me a reliable average? I mean really reliable, because this will be quite important."

So the next day Paul recorded the diameter of every reading taken, and took their average.

When Ben called, Paul read him the measurement. "Why that is tiny indeed. I was thinking of using a marble, but that's too big."

"For what, Ben?"

"Well, I'm going to sell our pet by rolling a ball bearing across the desk of every relevant military or civilian officer and telling him—here is the answer to all your problems!"

"Oh wow." Paul laughed. He understood Ben's careful wording—even on a secure line there could be problems, and this project was too potentially enormous in importance to risk it. Ben planned to scour the halls of the Pentagon, button holing any colonel or general in a blue uniform who was willing to listen. He'd roll a ball bearing across that officer's desk and tell him: "That's how big your stealth plane will be if you let us build it for you and support our efforts to get the contract or fill in the blanks."

Then the testing was done.

The answer would come in a few days: who had won the contract?

Chapter 34.

When Paul returned to the offices in Burbank, Ben was in a funk. Steve, too, was outraged. Paul, Ben Rich, and Steve Rossi were in Ben's office, with the door shut.

"This could be mucking disaster," raged Steve.

"Those SOBs!" Ben fulminated, banging his fist on his desk.

Steve explained: "Some civilian radar quack back east, 3000 miles away, has been sniping at us. We are now under investigation for possible fraud. Ben found out that the SOB who is in bed with companies that make electronic jamming devices that get installed planes to fool enemy radars. We could put his cronies out of business!

"But this clown has the ear of several generals back there, and they may favor Northrop because they are big and they've done business with them, whereas we are tiny and unknown to most Air Force blue-suiters."

"Well, why?" Paul asked in amazement.

"They say you falsified test results. That you may have done something to that pylon. We know that's nonsense because we tested it here and drew up the plans for you."

"Of course," Paul said. "Hah! So I'm under investigation again? Is Mr. Mandigar going to come walking in any minute with his attitude?"

Steve waved a hand. "No, no, this is much bigger. It's not about you, it's about the company. The top brass have been burning my phone with questions. Some of them can't believe we are as good as we are, much less that we might be beating the pants off Northrop."

The phone rang. Ben answered. Steve and Paul waited in quiet distress. "Oh really?" Ben boomed. "Okay then. Send him over. I'd love to. Tell him what I said. Thanks." Ben hung up and turned around with a grim smile. He folded his hands on his desk and announced: "I called your alma mater, Paul. Know a Dr. Lindsay Anderson?"

"Oh yes," Paul said. "Professor Anderson taught mathematical analysis at one time. I think I had him for a course, though he would remember me even less."

Dr. Anderson arrived at the plant the next day, a congenial gray-haired man in his 60's carrying a briefcase. After introductions to Paul and Steve in Ben's office, Anderson opened his briefcase and reached in. He pulled out a little sandwich baggie tied with a rubber band. In it were ball bearings.

"These are the little ones. The big ones are in the briefcase. I have a hard time believing your claims, but they will be easy to test. Got a magnetron?"

"We have a 10,000-watt test facility in the plant, and a 25,000-watt machine at our anechoic chamber in Rye Canyon."

"The ten k will do."

"Okay, Professor. We have the machine ready, and the model on it ready to test."

Anderson's testing was thorough and took all afternoon. First, he tested the integrity of the magnetometer itself by shooting several objects, including the D-21 mockup.

Then he shot the model of the Hopeless Diamond, with the same results encountered in all previous tests—almost zero return.

He gasped, scratched his hair, and shook his head sharply as if to clear it. "I feel like someone who doesn't believe in ghosts but has just seen one. You guys have a really weird effect here. Can you explain the principle?"

"Nossir," Steve said sharply. "That's going to be a closely guarded national defense secret."

"I understand," Anderson said. He opened his briefcase and pulled out a ball bearing the size of a golf ball. "Put this on top of the model and let's see the return."

Ten minutes later he said: "Outstanding. All I see is what looks like a golf ball."

Ben held out a twelve page typed report under see through plastic cover. "Here are the predicted results from our testing and also from White Sands. You may want to compare for consistency."

"Okay. Let's try the next size, which is one inch in diameter."

The result was a one inch ball showing in the radar screen.

Slowly and silently, the testing proceeded until all that resulted from shooting a 1/8 inch ball bearing glued to the skin of the model was a 1/8 inch return. "I think you have a fantastic technology here," Anderson said, closing his briefcase. "I will make my report to the Air Force, and I can assure you that I fully support your claims."

Ben, Steve, and Paul breathed a collective sigh of relief.

Within a week, the Air Force Chief of Staff himself called Ben to congratulate him on winning the competition.

The Hopeless Diamond had outdone its best competitor by ten times.

The Skunk Works was reaching by far the smallest radar returns ever achieved.

The new project name was now Have Blue, funded for nearly $30 million to produce two full-sized, fully functional Have Blue jet aircraft.

The Have Blue project was now the most highly secret project in the United States in thirty years, since the atomic bomb project during World War II!

Ben and Steve shook Paul's hand in congratulations. Ben told Paul: "I want you to go home and take a rest. Take a week off."

Paul started to protest, but Ben said: "No. I need you to rest up, because we're going to be up to our necks in this country's second Manhattan Project. Go home and forget about all this for a week. Go!"

Chapter 35.

As Paul drove home in the growing dark, with a light rain sprinkling the windshield, he felt drained.

After all the worry, the investigation, the hassles over the pylon, he'd won. His idea was going to make history. And yet he felt numb.

For the first time in months, he was alone with time on his hands. He thought about stopping for a bite to eat, but he wasn't that hungry. He'd make himself a can of chili and have a nice cold beer. He'd sit and watch television and just crap out. That was the ticket.

As he slowly neared his house, he sensed something different.

There was one car too many there.

He reached under the seat for a rag to wipe the condensed steam from inside the windshield. It was raining harder now, in gusts. A cold fresh wind crept through the slightly open vent window.

The Polanskis had a van and a sedan, but those were parked along the front of their house.

The car parked in front of Paul's house was unfamiliar.

As he pulled in beside the car, he shook his head. Maybe the Polanskis had visitors; but why park in his driveway rather than theirs?

Pulling his jacket over his head in the downpour, Paul dashed across the gravel driveway and up the wooden porch.

Key in hand, he was about to unlock the door.

"Hi," a strange woman said, stepping out of the shadows on the porch.

Paul nearly dropped the key at the sight of a thin, beautiful apparition.

"Paul."

He recognized Marsha's voice, but not Marsha.

"Marsha?"

She stepped forward awkwardly, fists tensed by her sides, her body language uncertain, almost scared. "I wanted to see you."

"It is you, isn't it?" He stepped closer for a look. This was a different Marsha. She was thinner and—

"One of the makeup people owed me a favor at one of the studios," she said with nervous, brittle humor. "I just cashed in some chips. They did my face and my hair. I also bought a new set of clothes." She wore an expensive dark brown leather jacket cut like a suit jacket, and a blouse and a pearl choker—the blouse had a thick, pearly look almost as rich as the pearl itself. She wore a dark brown miniskirt, dark hose through which her pale muscular calves glistened, and brown high heels. "I wanted to look my best."

"I'm stunned," he said, wondering why he felt no emotion one way or the other. "Well, are you staying somewhere in town?"

"No."

"If you'd like, come on in and I'll turn on the heat. I've been away most of this month."

"I know," she said walking awkwardly, stiffly, as if her high heeled shoes were too tight.

"How do you mean, you know?"

"Paul, think about the timing. This is no accident."

He closed the door. "I've had a hard month, and I think I'm hallucinating. Are you Marsha or not?" Somebody was playing a very grotesque prank on him. Was it Fitch getting back at him? Who was this razor-thin, hard beauty?

She shrugged her hands apart. "Paul, I'm Peter's mom, remember? We used to live next door." Her face took on an anguished expression. "Did I hurt you so badly that you forgot me?" She put her hands to her face. "I am such a fool."

Marsha would have burst into tears. This woman didn't. She strode to the door, her shoes echoing hard. "I should not have come. It was another mistake, and I'm sorry." She turned the handle and pulled the door open.

"Wait."

She turned, one foot on the door step. "What?"

"Why don't you sit down and I'll make tea."

"Are you sure?" She softened. "You look at me as if I were a stranger. It scares me. You're looking right through me, as if we'd never met before."

"I'm...lost for words."

She closed the door. "I'm sorry." She stepped close and put her hands on his shoulders. He recognized the hands—they were Marsha's. "You sit right down on the couch." He sat down, and she knelt down and pulled his shoes off, first one, then the other. "I'll make us some tea. Are you hungry?"

"A bit." He watched as she took off her jacket. "You've lost weight."

"I've been under stress too. And I've been working out, jogging. I've become a vegetarian."

"That your car out there?" He followed her into the kitchen, padding in his stocking feet. She kicked off the high heels and was beginning to look more and more like Marsha.

"I don't want to get my blouse dirty," she said. "Got an old shirt I can wear?"

"Yeah... let me see." He went into the bedroom, found a plain white T-shirt, smelled it to make sure it was clean, and brought it to her.

She pulled down the shades all around.

She took off her choker and laid it aside. She unbuttoned her blouse and took it off. Her body was slender and pale and different—more wiry, more athletic—if it had been hardened in a kiln. She reached behind, undid the fastener, and laid it on top of the blouse on a chair at the foot of the kitchen table.

Handing over the T-shirt, Paul recognized her round, firm breasts. Those were the pink nipples of Marsha that he had thought he'd never see again. "It is really you," he said.

She pulled the T-shirt over her head and shook it down to cover her upper body. It reached half way down her thighs. "I wanted to ask you a question, but I think it should wait until tomorrow."

"Are you staying here for the night?" Part of him wished she wouldn't.

"Unless you want me to sleep in my car."

"No. I don't want that."

"Honey," she said, "I had no idea it would be like this." She stepped close and held his face between her palms. Her fingers were cold. "If you want, I'll walk out of here tonight. If you want to be rid of me. I wouldn't blame you." She regarded him with big serious eyes. "There has not been anyone else, you should know that. Not even a kiss on a date, Paul."

"Me neither."

"I know."

"What do you mean, you know?"

She laughed. "Mr. Rich told me you've been up to your eyeballs in nose cones."

"You've been talking to Ben Rich?"

"I called them to ask if I can have my old job back. They fell all over themselves because I said I'll settle my suit and we're done."

"You want to come back to Burbank?" His stomach twisted. It had been better when she was totally gone.

"Maybe. Will you do me a great favor?"

"Sure."

She took his hands in hers. "I know I don't deserve it, and you certainly must be honest and say no if you feel that way, but would you please try to put up with me for a day or two?" She misted a little. Her voice got thick. "I just thought—."

She started to rummage around, making dinner. Paul took a cola out—no beer; he wanted to have a clear head. While she cooked—macaroni and cheese from a box, toast, a can of artichokes—"you need someone to go shop for you"—he sat at the kitchen table with his cola and watched her.

"How is Pete?"

"Pete is fine. He's with Jeffrey's parents, and they are having a ball with him."

"So you were right. It was good to go back home."

"Yes it was. And then it wasn't. Something came up."

"What was that?"

"I'll tell you tomorrow, okay?"

He shrugged. He was still numb, and he was shocked at how he felt nothing. She could have walked out right now, and he would have gone about his business of feeling sad and lonely without skipping a beat. But he wouldn't tell her that, because he wasn't a mean person, and it was okay after these months.

She looked cute in that T-shirt, the dark little skirt, the dark hose covering a very fine pair of legs.

"So you called Steve and he said you could have your job back."

"Yes."

"What else did you and Steve talk about?"

She put plates on the table.

"Want help?"

"No, just sit." She brushed her fingertips behind his ear and went for the silverware. Rattling knives and forks onto the table, she said: "I asked Ben how you were."

Paul shrugged. "How would he know how I am?"

She brought the pan over and spooned out macaroni. "He said that you seemed very sad after I left."

"How would he know?" Paul waved his hands in the air.

"Because he could see how fond you were of Peter and me." She slid his plate in front of him and sat down. She picked at her food while he ate in a steady rhythm. "He knew you were hurting."

Paul said: "Tell me about Pete."

"Pete is in school up there and doing fine. He has some new friends who come over to play with Condor IV. He tells them all about his great friend Paul who works for the Government. He's quite proud of you. And he misses you."

"I got his little note not long ago."

"He wished you'd answer it, but I understand—."

Paul was silent. He couldn't carry on a relationship with her son while she dumped him. If she wanted to contact him, she should do it directly, not through her son. But she hadn't.

After dinner, she did the dishes while he hung out in the kitchen. He did feel the compulsion to hover around her.

When she was done, she dried her hands on a dish towel. "Do you want me to spend the night?"

"Yes."

She smiled. "Okay, then I'm going to change. I'll be back in a few minutes. Mind if I take a shower?"

"Of course not."

He watched the news on the TV in the living room.

A while later she came through the house in her familiar nightgown. On her feet were the fuzzy slipper that went flop, flop, flop.

"It is you," he said.

"It is me," she agreed. "Are you tired?"

"Very."

"How about we slip into bed and just pillow talk?"

Soon, they were in bed and the room was dark except for soft stray light from the street light down the road. She felt warm beside him. The rain fell quietly and steadily outside, beading the windows, a rare desert rain that made the air smell fresh. She laid her cheek on his shoulder, snuggled very close with one leg wrapped around his thigh, and sighed. "I dreamed about this," she said.

He touched her cheek, and kissed her scalp through her hair. It smelled kind of fresh and clean, and he remembered her coconut smell.

"That was nice," she said. "That's the first time you've kissed me."

"Oh, so you want to be kissed."

"Yes." She kissed his cheek and hovered, waiting, staring over the hillside of his cheek. He reached around her, feeling the incredible smoothness and the music in the curvature of her body. He pulled her to him. She was hungry, her breath hot as she sought his mouth with hers like a starving animal. Her strong hand grasped his face as her tongue forced itself in to his mouth and she leverage herself on top of him.

Then he grasped her in his much stronger arms and rolled over, pinning her underneath him. Her knees were pulled up into his ribs and her hands grasped his buttocks, pulling him toward her. "Yes," she said, "now."

They slept late into the next day, awakening every few hours to make love.

About noon, they lay tiredly and playfully nuzzling as warm sunshine poured in under a closed shade.

"I'm sorry about what happened," she told him, thoughtfully twirling a few strands of his hair over his forehead with her fingers.

"Funny thing," he said, "I was really hurt, but I buried myself in my work, and when Ben kicked me out yesterday and made me take a week off, I was terrified that I would finally have to deal with my feelings."

She nodded. "Honey, Steve did just the right thing. When I asked how you were, he knew the score. He said, *Are you coming back?* And I said *Maybe*—because I've done nothing but think about you, more and more lately. There isn't another you in this whole world. See, I thought I didn't love you because I didn't feel about you the way I felt about Jeffrey. But I can never meet him again or feel that way. I feel differently about you, but it's just as strong in a deeper way, because I was a girl when I fell in love with Jeffrey, and now I'm a woman and I'm in love for the second time in my life. Well anyway, Mr. Rich said, *Do you want to know when would be the best time to talk with him?* I said, *Yes, if you don't tell him we talked.* He said *I'll let you know as soon as we finish this big project in the next week or two, and I'll tell you exactly when to be sitting on his doorstep.* "

"Clever timing," Paul agreed.

She smiled fondly, running her finger over the contour of his cheek. "He said, Let's make a deal. You wait so he doesn't get all rattled before we're done, and I'll make him stay home a week so you two can work out whatever you're going to do. "

Paul shook his head and laughed. "All that time, he knew you wanted to see me, and I was aching inside from losing you?"

She nodded.

"You said you were going to ask me a question, but you would wait until today."

"Yes. Want me to ask?"

"Okay, go ahead."

"Do you love me?"

"Yes."

"You weren't so sure yesterday."

"I'm just getting over the shock."

"You're not going to resent me?"

"No. You see, because I didn't deal with my pain, it never was an issue."

She tore her hair and shook her head, rolling her eyes. "Men!"

"So," he concluded, "right now I feel as if the last few months never happened, and you just went away for a little vacation."

"Honestly? How do guys do that?"

"It's top secret, like nose cones." He wiggled the tip of her nose.

Epilog

This novel is a work of historical fiction.

The Have Blue project was a historical fact.

On 16 November 1977, a Galaxy C5-A transport aircraft landed at Burbank Airport. The first operational stealth plane, HB 1001, was loaded on board and flown to Groom Lake for testing. HB 1002 followed soon after. Both planes were lost during testing (both pilots ejecting safely). This was the end of the Have Blue project, which confirmed the flight worthiness of the unique flight design of the F-117A, as well as the success of its radar evasion capabilities. Stealth technology was rapidly becoming a key part of our national arsenal, and the proven concept now was on its way to becoming functional military hardware.

During the 1980 presidential debate, candidates Jimmy Carter and Ronald Reagan both mentioned a mysterious technology vital to our national interest, called stealth, and the press pursued eagerly any crumbs of information that might fall off the table. Ronald Reagan became president and the nation's rearmament proceeded full tilt in great secrecy. Mysteriously, rumors appeared about various 'black' (highly secret) projects including one called Aurora and another called Manta. Conspiracy theorists hovering outside government testing areas began to report all sorts of strange sightings and gave enormous new impetus to all sorts of UFO theories. Anyone who blundered near the facilities was interrogated by Federal officials and frightened within an inch of their lives—more fodder for conspiracy theories. The interrogators themselves had no idea what they were protecting—one allegedly thought the Air Force was building a time machine (Robert Dorr reporting in Lockheed F-117 Nighthawk, Aerospace Publishing Ltd., London U.K. and Westport, Conn. U.S.A. 1995).

The squadron was camouflaged by the cover of operational fighter planes including Vought A-7D's at Nevada's Tonopah Test Range during the early 1980's. Operations were so secret that the planes were said to fly only on nights of little or no moon (as during their initial combat deployment over Iraq a decade later). Of special concern were the Soviet spy satellites that moved daily over U.S. facilities with incredibly high resolution cameras. Lockheed was adept at playing games with the Soviets, to the extent of moving cars around in parking lots and changing designated parking spots to prevent the Soviets from knowing who was in the plant at a given hour. The same rationale drove the parking of A-7D fighters around the F-117A hangars.

While the F117A was becoming a military reality, testing and deployment were advancing on an even more sophisticated warplane, the B-2 stealth bomber. Computer technology had, by the 1980's, advanced sufficiently that designers could go beyond the mathematically simple triangles of Have Blue and actually plot curved surfaces requiring many billions of calculations to perfect. These curved surfaces are evident in the B-2's unusual design.

The F-117A is not really a fighter, but a bomber. It carries two laser-guided 2,000 pound smart bombs especially designed for its bomb bay. It is a sizeable bomb, at the lower end of the spectrum of so-called block busters, and its precision guidance means the bomb can be pinpoint targeted. This caused the F-117A to contribute enormously during the Gulf War in 1990 and also during the NATO bombing campaign over Yugoslavia in 1999.

The crash of an F-117A near Bakersfield, California, on 11 July 1986 began to really blow off the lid of secrecy. In the tragedy, pilot Maj. Ross E. Mulhare was killed. Security police cordoned off the area and would not even let local firefighters approach to battle a 150-acre blaze amid dry brush.

On 14 October 1987 a second F-117A crashed at Nellis AFB, killing its pilot, Maj. Michael C. Stewart.

In October 1988, the Pentagon is said to have begun leaking information about its stealth fighter, just weeks before national elections, to give George Bush a boost over Michael Dukakis (Robert F. Dorr, op. cit.). The leaks were confirmed days after the election, on 10 November 1988, when Secretary of Defense J. Daniel Howard held a news conference announcing the plane's operational readiness, and showing a single blurred photo that hid the plane's faceted design.

The Lockheed F-117A stealth fighter was initiated into combat during Operation Just Cause in Panama, in December 1989, for the ouster of narco-dictator Manuel Noriega. The aircraft saw only minor action.

When Operation Desert Storm was launched in August 1990, the F-117A found its greatest hours of glory, taking out targets in downtown Baghdad with surgical precision. The U.S. Air Force would claim that the F-117A craft were only 2.5% of fighting aircraft present in theater, but that they hit about 40% of the targets struck during the war.

During the bombing of Yugoslavia in 1999, one F-117A was lost to ground AA fire at night, and one proposed explanation was that the sophisticated Soviet-era tracking systems were able to locate it and track its flight through smooth coordination among a chain of tracking stations. By this time the diamond technology was aging, and in any case little could be gained from the materials on the ground alone without the calculations needed for the skin configuration. The pilot was rescued during one of the most spectacular night rescues by a helicopter crew ever.

Various proposals were in the works for successor models at the time of publication (October 1999).

Most of the characters in this work of historical fiction (Paul Owens, the Kassners, Steve Rossi) are fictional indeed. Some, like Ben Rich, Bill Schroeder, and others aren't. One of the most central figures in the real history is not mentioned—Denys Overholser, whom Ben Rich credits with initially connecting Pyotr Ufimtsev's paper with stealth design which Bill Schroeder then brought into full mathematical fruition.

This novel is an entertainment, and in no way reflects on the lives and personalities of real people mentioned in the historical events. As a work of historical fiction, it takes liberties in creating personalities around real events. The author wishes to point the reader to his sources, so that the reader can fully appreciate the true dramatic story of the Stealth Fighter's development. As mentioned earlier, the primary source of information has been the nonfiction book "Skunk Works : A Personal Memoir of My Years at Lockheed" by Ben R. Rich with Leo Janos, Little Brown and Co., 1996. Other references include: "Lockheed F-117 Nighthawk" by Robert F. Dorr, Aerospace Publishing Ltd., London U.K. and Westport Conn U.S.A. 1995; "F117 Stealth in action" by Jim Goodall, Squadron/Signal Publications Inc., Carrollton, TX U.S.A. 1991; "Lockheed Horizons" ed. Thomas J. Goff, Lockheed Creative Communications, Calabasas CA U.S.A., Issue No. 30, May 1992.

HAVE BLUE

by John Argo

A Romantic Techno-Thriller based on true history

More Info: Clocktower Books

= online since 1996 =

Clocktower Books was, to our knowledge, the world's first publisher ever to publish real digital, proprietary (not public domain), novel-length fiction (books, novels) online in digital format for download. We launched this program in 1996, using an innovative process of publishing weekly serial chapters. Readers who needed to know the outcome, and couldn't stand the suspense, could email for a complete digital text file anywhere in the world. We received raves and kudos from around the globe. We used this serial chapter method to publish three John Argo books over 1996-1996: *This Shoal of Space* and *Pioneers* (both SF); and *Neon Blue*, a suspense novel. All three novels were bestsellers in the earliest e-book forums, including the original Barnes & Noble website in 2000, and other venues including Rocket eBooks. See the publisher website for more info:

www.clocktowerbooks.com

More Info: John Argo @ Café Okay

John Argo is a writer of sentimental fiction, be it a romantic techno-thriller like *Have Blue*, or novels of speculative and dark fiction .He lives with his wife and family in Southern California.

Whenever you read a John Argo story or novel, no matter how dark or thrilling, you will almost always also find a love story.

John Argo's web presence is at Clocktower Books, online and publishing full, proprietary e-book novels since 1996. Visit his new Web venture (2015 forward) at :

www.cafeokay.com

www.ingramcontent.com/pod-product-compliance
Lightning Source LLC
Chambersburg PA
CBHW051826170626
46807CB00003B/1047